CATASTROPHE IN A CLOISTER

(A Lacey Doyle Cozy Mystery—Book Nine)

FIONA GRACE

Fiona Grace

Fiona Grace is author of the LACEY DOYLE COZY MYSTERY series, comprising nine books; of the TUSCAN VINEYARD COZY MYSTERY series, comprising six books; of the DUBIOUS WITCH COZY MYSTERY series, comprising three books; of the BEACHFRONT BAKERY COZY MYSTERY series, comprising six books; and of the CATS AND DOGS COZY MYSTERY series, comprising six books.

Fiona would love to hear from you, so please visit www.fionagraceauthor.com to receive free ebooks, hear the latest news, and stay in touch.

ISBN: 978-1-0943-8151-0

BOOKS BY FIONA GRACE

LACEY DOYLE COZY MYSTERY

MURDER IN THE MANOR (Book#1)
DEATH AND A DOG (Book #2)
CRIME IN THE CAFE (Book #3)
VEXED ON A VISIT (Book #4)
KILLED WITH A KISS (Book #5)
PERISHED BY A PAINTING (Book #6)
SILENCED BY A SPELL (Book #7)
FRAMED BY A FORGERY (Book #8)
CATASTROPHE IN A CLOISTER (Book #9)

TUSCAN VINEYARD COZY MYSTERY

AGED FOR MURDER (Book #1)
AGED FOR DEATH (Book #2)
AGED FOR MAYHEM (Book #3)
AGED FOR SEDUCTION (Book #4)
AGED FOR VENGEANCE (Book #5)
AGED FOR ACRIMONY (Book #6)

DUBIOUS WITCH COZY MYSTERY

SKEPTIC IN SALEM: AN EPISODE OF MURDER (Book #1)
SKEPTIC IN SALEM: AN EPISODE OF CRIME (Book #2)
SKEPTIC IN SALEM: AN EPISODE OF DEATH (Book #3)

BEACHFRONT BAKERY COZY MYSTERY

BEACHFRONT BAKERY: A KILLER CUPCAKE (Book #1)
BEACHFRONT BAKERY: A MURDEROUS MACARON (Book #2)
BEACHFRONT BAKERY: A PERILOUS CAKE POP (Book #3)
BEACHFRONT BAKERY: A DEADLY DANISH (Book #4)
BEACHFRONT BAKERY: A TREACHEROUS TART (Book #5)
BEACHFRONT BAKERY: A CALAMITOUS COOKIE (Book #6)

CATS AND DOGS COZY MYSTERY

A VILLA IN SICILY: OLIVE OIL AND MURDER (Book #1)
A VILLA IN SICILY: FIGS AND A CADAVER (Book #2)

A VILLA IN SICILY: VINO AND DEATH (Book #3)
A VILLA IN SICILY: CAPERS AND CALAMITY (Book #4)
A VILLA IN SICILY: ORANGE GROVES AND VENGEANCE (Book #5)
A VILLA IN SICILY: CANNOLI AND A CASUALTY (Book #6)

CHAPTER ONE

"It's going to snow tomorrow," Gina said, turning from the dark view out of the kitchen window of Crag Cottage to face Lacey. "I'm sure of it."

Lacey tucked a brown curl behind her ear. "You've been saying that every day since New Year's," she retorted.

"Well this time, I'm right," her gray-haired friend replied, adjusting her red-framed spectacles as she glanced back out the window. "I just saw a squirrel burying an acorn."

Lacey tutted affectionately at her older friend's penchant for superstition. "I'm starting to think you want a white wedding more than I do…"

In just a few days' time, Lacey was tying the knot with her fiancé, Tom, and Gina, her maid of honor, was being even more crazy than usual about the last-minute preparations. Her most recent anxiety was over whether it would snow or not. Since the theme of the wedding was Winter Wonderland, Lacey would of course love it if it snowed, but she wasn't about to get stressed over something she had no control over. Gina, on the other hand…

"We should do another wedding dress fitting," her friend suddenly exclaimed, jumping back from the window and swirling to face Lacey.

"I did one yesterday," Lacey replied.

"Yes, but it's better to do small adjustments now rather than wait until the actual day to find out we need to do a big one."

Lacey smirked. "Is this your way of telling me I'm putting on weight?"

Gina put her hands on her hips. "Lacey. Please. Just try the dress on again. For me."

"Fine," Lacey replied with a sigh. "I'll be right back."

She headed out of the quaint country-style kitchen and along the dark, low-ceilinged corridor to the staircase opposite the wooden front door. The steps creaked as she ascended, passing the many antique artworks she'd collected over the past year.

She didn't mind trying on the dress again really. The beautiful gown was a one of a kind, handmade, antique redesign; the result of some secretive scheming between her father, Gina, and Taryn from the boutique next door to Lacey's store. It couldn't be more perfect for a vintage-lover like Lacey, and trying it on always made her feel like a million bucks.

She went into the large master bedroom at the front of the house, where long white lace curtains hung either side of the beautiful French doors that opened onto the balcony. As she trotted inside, Chester, her English shepherd, stirred from his slumber at the foot of her four-poster bed. He raised his head, blinked at her, and yawned deeply.

"You and me both, Chester," Lacey said, catching his yawn and yawning herself. "Wedding prep is exhausting." She went over to the beechwood closet. "I swear these days I wake up tired."

She pulled open the closet doors, revealing the gorgeous wedding dress in all its glory, and let out a sigh of admiration.

Just think, in a few days, she'd be married to Tom! It was so close now, she was starting to feel queasy with nerves. Which was understandable, given her complicated family history.

Speaking of family, Lacey headed over to her bedside dresser and checked the calendar. Her mom, sister, and nephew, Frankie, were due to fly here in two days, and she was a bundle of nerves about it. It was their first face-to-face meeting since Lacey had dropped the bombshell on them that she'd tracked down their long-lost father, Frank. She suspected there would be some difficult conversations ahead, though of course nothing would be more awkward than the moment they all reunited. She'd made some careful plans for that moment, by booking a table at a comfortable restaurant a little off the beaten track. The place wasn't overly stuffy or informal, and the tables were more like booths, which would give them at least some semblance of privacy from prying eyes during the inevitable raised voices and heated discussions.

Lacey pushed the thoughts out of her mind and took the dress over to the vanity mirror. Her hair had grown quite long now, ever since the rebelliously short style she'd had cut on her first days in Wilfordshire, and it hung in dark curls over her shoulders. She slipped out of her day clothes and into the wedding dress. Just like the day she'd first tried it on, it fit perfectly.

"See," Lacey said to Chester. "I told Gina I hadn't put on any weight!"

Chester snorted through his nostrils, then laid his head back down on his paws and closed his eyes. But as Lacey turned back to her reflection, a fresh wave of nausea washed over her. So much for pushing her family worries out of her mind.

She smoothed her hands down the fabric, taking deep breaths to settle her nerves.

"Lacey!" Gina called from the kitchen. "Where are you?"

"Just coming," she called back.

At last the sick feeling passed. Lacey gathered up her dress with both hands to stop it from dragging on the floorboards and headed back out of the bedroom door. She began her slow, careful descent down the staircase, feeling a bit like a debutante at a ball as she took one slow, cautious step at a time.

But when she was halfway down the staircase, she suddenly heard a sound.

Her head darted up and her eyes found Tom, paused halfway through the open front doorway, key still in the lock, gazing at her with his mouth agape and a stunned look in his light green eyes.

"Tom!" Lacey screamed, aghast, gathering up the dress and racing in an ungainly fashion back up the staircase. "You're not supposed to see the dress until the wedding! It's bad luck!"

She reached the landing, her heart thumping, and pressed her back to the wall. It wasn't so much her own superstition that she was worried about, but Gina's. Gina was notorious for bad omens. Once she got an idea in her head, she rarely let it go, and the last thing Lacey wanted right now was another reason for her maid of honor to stress.

"Sorry!" Tom's voice floated up the staircase to her. "I didn't actually see much. Or anything. I—er—I didn't see anything!"

Lacey knew he was only saying that for her sake. He'd quite clearly gotten a good look. And whether it was Gina rubbing off on her or her own superstitions, Lacey felt a sudden niggle of worry in her chest. She'd already been feeling anxious about the family reunion, and now she felt even worse.

She raced back into her room—Chester harrumphing at the second intrusion to his slumber—and quickly changed back into her normal clothes. Then she hurried back downstairs, bracing herself for whatever Gina was about to unleash.

She entered the kitchen, stepping down the step onto the ochre tiles. Tom, dressed casually in a pair of jeans and gray T-shirt that showed off his golden-hued arms, was cowering beside the Aga, framed by the dark window, with Gina standing in front of him like some kind of schoolteacher mid-scold. Lacey could tell this was going to be bad.

"Good news," Lacey said nervously, forcing out a breezy voice as she crossed the tiles toward them, "I haven't put on ten pounds since yesterday…"

But her attempt at light-hearted joviality did not work. Gina swirled on the spot and glowered at her.

"Is it true?" she demanded. "Did Tom just see you in your dress?"

"I was looking at my phone," Tom said, hurriedly. "I only caught a glimpse."

"A glimpse is still a glimpse!" Gina cried. "It's very bad luck!"

"Gina, please," Lacey warned. "Don't make a big deal out of this. I am already nervous enough as it is, what with Mom and Dad about to meet face to face for the first time in thirty years. I don't need you adding to it with talk of bad omens!"

"I don't make the rules," Gina retorted. "I just point out the signs. And that's one of the worst, Lacey!"

Lacey was about to refute that when at that very moment, the phone began to ring. The uncanny timing and the sudden shrill interruption of their conversion made everyone freeze—even Tom, who didn't have a superstitious bone in his body.

The three of them exchanged glances.

"I told you!" Gina cried. "I'll bet that's something bad."

"Gina!" Lacey hissed, shuddering.

Tom started to chuckle, showing off his lovely straight pearly white teeth as he did. "Come on, now. It's just coincidental timing. It's probably a cold caller. No one else calls at this time of the evening."

His words didn't make Lacey feel particularly reassured. Tom clearly thought Gina was off her rocker, which meant Lacey, by default, was a fool for even entertaining her.

As Lacey hurried across the kitchen toward the ringing phone, Gina shook her head of frizzy gray hair.

"It's already beginning," she muttered, ominously.

"Nothing's beginning!" Lacey exclaimed, glaring over her shoulder at her friend.

She reached the telephone and picked it up. But despite her bravado, her voice quavered as she spoke. "He—hello?"

"Is that Lacey Doyle?" the voice on the other end asked, a male voice that was croaky with age.

"Yes…" Lacey said.

"And you're an auctioneer?"

Lacey drew her brows together. Her home phone was set up to get diverted calls from the store when it was closed for business, but as of yet, she'd never actually received one. Most people just waited until the next day to call about their queries. She wondered what was so urgent that this man had decided he needed to speak to her off-hours.

"That's right," she replied.

"My name is Abbot Weeks of St. Cyril's Abbey."

An Abbot? Lacey thought with surprise, her mind going straight to horror movies and creepy old monasteries. Now *that* certainly felt ominous.

"How can I help you, Abbot Weeks?" she asked, forcing her voice to stay level.

From where they were watching on, Gina's and Tom's eyes widened. Gina looked like the world was ending, while Tom looked thoroughly entertained.

"I have a very urgent matter I need your help with," Abbot Weeks said in her ear.

Lacey felt herself begin to tremble. "And what would that be?"

"It's not something I feel comfortable speaking to you over the telephone about, but it's regarding an antique. Would you be able to come here so we can talk about it further? Tomorrow?"

Lacey floundered. She was supposed to be going through wedding things with Gina tomorrow—not because they were necessary, per se, but because Gina had insisted on it. Yet this sounded so intriguing. She couldn't help the spark of curiosity igniting inside of her. Besides, St. Cyril's Abbey was only a couple hours outside of Wilfordshire. It wouldn't take too much time out of her day.

She flicked open her diary and saw that almost every spare inch had been written on. She grimaced as her eyes glanced over all the wedding-related dates—flight times and hotel details of various guests flying in from the states, invoice payment dues for the caterers and musicians, rehearsals, breakfast, photo shoot—until she spotted the smallest slither of space. Her eyes lit up with excitement.

"I can certainly squeeze you in tomorrow," she said. "What time would it be?"

From her peripheral vision she saw Gina's face drop. Then her friend came marching toward her, hands on hips. She was clearly going for the phone, and Lacey had no choice but to turn her back on her and cradle the phone before she got a chance to yank it from her and slam it down.

"Whenever suits you," Abbot Weeks replied. "As soon as you're able."

"Perfect," Lacey said, turning on the spot as Gina grappled for the phone. "The morning would be best for me."

"Wonderful. I look forward to seeing you. Oh, and please come alone. This must remain secret."

"Alone?" Lacey echoed with a flutter of apprehension. "Yes, that's fine. Goodbye."

She put down the phone and disengaged herself from the tangle of Gina's arms. Her friend was red-faced with exasperation. Behind her, Tom, on the other hand, appeared to be thoroughly amused.

"Lacey!" Gina cried. "Please don't tell me you just agreed to go to a monastery *alone*?"

"It was too good an opportunity to turn down," Lacey admitted. "It's not every day I get a call from a monk requesting an urgent visit about some secret antique he can't discuss over the telephone!"

Gina stared at her, aghast. "This is bad," she fretted, pacing away and wringing her hands. "Very, very bad."

"Please don't worry," Lacey said. "I'll have Chester with me. He can protect me."

Gina swirled on the spot. "Not from ghosts, he can't! Not from curses and omens! Oh Lacey, I really think you should give this one a miss. However exciting it may sound. I just don't have a good feeling about it."

Lacey knew better than to entertain Gina's anxieties, but that didn't mean they didn't worm their way into her mind. Maybe going to the monastery tomorrow was a bad idea.

She caught Tom's eye. He gave her a little shrug. At least he thought Gina was overreacting and worrying about nothing.

Well, there was only one way to find out who was right, Lacey decided, and that was to go to St. Cyril's Abbey tomorrow and find out.

CHAPTER TWO

Lacey awoke to a frigidly cold, misty morning and hurried to the window to discover the world shrouded by fog. But there wasn't a single flake of snow in sight.

"Aha!" she announced to Chester, as he snored at the end of the bed. "See! Gina's whole squirrel burying acorn superstition was wrong. And if she can be wrong about that, she can be wrong about the monastery trip being a bad omen."

Chester opened an eye, regarded her, then closed it again. Tom, still snuggled up under the covers, stirred.

"What?" he asked, groggily, opening his eyes to slits. "Did you just say something about squirrels?"

Lacey chuckled. "I was just talking to Chester, my dear. You go back to sleep."

"Okay," Tom replied with a yawn, pulling the duvet right up to his ears and promptly falling straight back to sleep.

Poor Tom rarely got a morning off from his patisserie, and whenever he did, he was practically dead to the world.

Lacey smiled to herself contentedly and skipped to the en suite for her morning shower. As warm water beat down on her, she thought again about how Gina's snow prediction was wrong. And if that was wrong, then surely the bad omen was wrong as well.

As she allowed herself to relax, she began to grow excited about the meeting with the abbot later today. She simply couldn't resist the temptation of a mystery! What could the highly secretive meeting be all about? What kind of antique might a monk from a monastery have to show her?

Growing increasingly excited, Lacey rushed through her morning routine. She dressed herself for the cold weather in jeans and a gray knit sweater, then trotted down into the kitchen to down her usual shot of black espresso and feed Chester his breakfast.

As she began pouring kibble out of the big paper bag into Chester's bowl, she heard a knock on the wooden stable back door. There was only one person with access to her back door, and that was Gina, who lived next door. She set the bulky bag down, leaving Chester to chow on his breakfast, and unlatched the door. She pulled it open and smiled at her friend standing on the step, all bundled up and shivering in her winter coat.

"Morning!" Lacey trilled.

Before Gina had a chance to reply, her elderly English shepherd, Boudica, came charging inside the kitchen. She promptly stuck her nose straight into Chester's bowl and nudged him out of the way.

"Boo! You greedy mare!" Gina exclaimed. "You've already had your breakfast!"

Lacey chuckled. Of the two dogs, Boudica was the boss.

Gina wiped her wellies on the welcome mat and stepped inside, letting out a theatrical shiver. "Chilly morning, huh?" she said.

"Chilly indeed," Lacey replied, leadingly. "And yet… no snow."

Gina gave her a look. "So *that's* why you're so chipper, is it? You think you're off the hook because my snow prediction didn't come true?"

Lacey simply grinned cheekily at her friend.

She grabbed Chester's leash and her winter jacket off the coat hooks and laced on her leather boots, and then they all headed out together for the misty walk to work.

They took the cliff path onto the beach. Though the longer route, it was the more pleasant, and the dogs loved it. As soon as their feet hit the sand, the dogs streaked off across it, snapping their jaws at the gray waves as they broke on the shore.

The beach looked particularly eerie in the dawn light, and there was no one else around, making it spookier still.

Gina shivered beside Lacey. "I don't know about you, but I really don't have a good feeling about this fog. You know what they say about fog, don't you?"

Lacey rolled her eyes affectionately. "No. What do they say about fog?"

Gina spoke in a conspiratorial tone. *"Fog in the hollow, fine day to follow; fog on the hill, water to the mill…"*

Lacey looked at her with a curious frown. "And what does that mean, exactly?"

Gina shrugged. "I don't know, but it's definitely not good. I think you should call off the trip to the monastery."

Lacey shook her head. "Absolutely not. I'm not passing up such an intriguing mystery just because of some mist."

"All right, all right, but superstitions aside, it's your wedding that's the real issue! We're meant to be going through the itinerary this morning."

"The trip won't take long," Lacey assured her. "I'll be back by this afternoon. We can do the itinerary then."

Gina simply harrumphed.

They reached the Coach House—the gorgeous brick pub that stood on the corner between the promenade road and the high street—and turned onto the cobblestone street. Wilfordshire High Street was just waking up, with its various quaint stores opening for the day. The Christmas lights were still strung from lamppost to lamppost, along with the town's white and blue winter bunting.

"When do they take down the lights?" Lacey asked Gina.

"January sixth," Gina replied without missing a beat. "It's bad luck to keep decorations up past then."

Lacey chuckled. Of course.

They walked past the terraced store fronts with their bulging bay windows, heading for the antiques store. They'd almost made it when a shrill voice came up from behind.

"Lacey! Oh, Lacey!"

Lacey tensed. It was the trilling voice of Taryn.

Ever since she'd made Lacey's wedding dress, Taryn had been fishing for an invite to the wedding. Lacey wasn't sure why she was so desperate to come considering how much she clearly hated her, and could only presume it was to show off—or worse, to show Lacey up! Lacey wouldn't put anything past Taryn. She'd made some low blows in the past.

Still, Lacey felt bad for her and was going to invite her eventually. She was just putting off telling her because she was enjoying having Taryn be ingratiating for a while, and suspected her demeanor would change just as soon as she got what she wanted.

"Morning, Taryn," Lacey said, politely, as she took the store key from her pocket and operated the mechanical shutters. "How are you today?"

"Very well, thank you," Taryn replied, raising her voice to be heard over the noisy sound of the rattling metal. "Though I'm not so sure about this fog. Fog always gives me a bad feeling."

"Thank you!" Gina exclaimed.

"Not you as well," Lacey muttered.

"Not me as well, what?" Taryn asked, her over-plucked brows turning inward as she frowned.

"Gina's been going on about all kinds of weather-related superstitions," Lacey explained. "Squirrels and acorns and fog on the mill."

"Tom accidentally saw her in her wedding dress," Gina explained.

Taryn gasped theatrically. "Oh no! That's a terrible omen."

"That's what I'm trying to tell her."

The shutters clicked into their open position, and Lacey put her key in the store lock. "There's not much I can do about it now, is there?" she said. "What's happened has happened."

"You could cancel your trip," Gina said.

"You're going on a trip?" Taryn cried, as if this was the worst news in the world.

"A *day* trip!" Lacey exclaimed. The lock yielded and she pushed the door open. "And it's going to be fine." But as she looked over her shoulder at them, she spotted a black cat streaking across the cobblestones. With less certainty, she added, "I'm sure of it."

She entered the store, the other two women coming in after her. The dogs rushed past their legs to get to the prime slumbering spot first. Despite her arthritic knees, Boudica still got there first and lay down with a pleased look on her face, leaving poor Chester to take the lesser favored spot beside her.

"I'll get the coffee on, shall I?" Gina said, heading for the archway that led to the backrooms. "Taryn? Are you staying for coffee?"

"Oh go on then," Taryn said. "You've twisted my arm."

It had become something of an unspoken tradition now, that on Monday morning Taryn would pop around and stay for a coffee.

But the thought of another coffee made Lacey queasy. She paused in the middle of the store as a wave of sickness went over her.

"Actually, can I have something milder?" she asked Gina. "A peppermint tea? Something to settle my stomach. All this wedding stress is making me feel quite nauseous."

"Wedding stress…" Gina said, pausing beneath the arch and giving Lacey a suspicious look, "…or a bad omen…" Then she disappeared under the arch and out of view.

Taryn looked over from the shelf of antique pottery she'd been idly perusing to Lacey. "Or maybe you're pregnant?"

Taryn had quite clearly meant it as a joke, but her comment made Lacey freeze. Because now she thought about it she realized she was, indeed, late. She'd been so wrapped up in the wedding preparations and stress over the family reunion she'd not been keeping track of those particular dates.

Cold dread washed over her. Her mind began racing. Could she actually be pregnant? Was that why she'd been experiencing waves of nausea? Had she attributed to stress something that was in fact a symptom of something else?

With panic fluttering in her chest, Lacey realized there was only one way to know for certain. She'd have to get a test. And suddenly, that was all she cared about, like her mind had laser focused on it.

"What's wrong with you?" Taryn asked, interrupting her ruminations. "I mean, are you all right?" she amended, evidently remembering she was trying to be more pleasant these days. "You've gone pale. Are you sick?"

"I'm fine," Lacey said, quickly. "I just… thought of something… I forgot to do this morning. An errand I need to run." She was starting to feel panicky and vulnerable under the notoriously nosy Taryn's scrutiny. She needed to get out right now. "The bank!" she cried, thinking up the first excuse she could.

Taryn looked confused. "The bank doesn't open till nine."

Crap, Lacey thought. Not only was her cover story full of holes, but Taryn's comment had reminded her that the pharmacy, like the bank, did not open until nine. She'd have to wait until after her monastery meeting to buy a test. How was she going to get through the meeting with Abbot Weeks while this was percolating away in the back of her mind?

"Right, yes," Lacey said. "But I don't need to go *into* the bank, I just need to deposit some checks in that safety drop-off thing outside."

"I wouldn't trust that," Taryn said, knowingly. "It looks like a laundry chute to me. Posting a check? Seems far too risky!" She put her hands on her hips. "And besides, who's paying you with checks? That's not very sensible, Lacey. What if they bounce? That might be how you do things in America, but over here you really need to use chip and pin."

"I'll—er—I'll bear that in mind," Lacey said rapidly. "Chester! Chester, come on, boy, let's go!"

Chester jumped up and followed Lacey as she hurried for the exit, her mind a swirl of anxiety. Just as she reached the door, she heard the clinking sound of crockery coming from behind.

"Lacey?" Gina called. "You're leaving already? But I just made your tea! And you don't need to leave for the monastery yet."

Lacey pulled the door open. "Errands!" she cried over her shoulder without looking back.

And with Chester on her heel, she hurried away.

CHAPTER THREE

Lacey had a lot of thoughts swirling in her mind during the drive to the monastery. So much so she barely noticed the beautiful British countryside as it passed by outside her window. Winter had turned the trees bare and the fields barren, giving it the sort of romantic, bleak beauty Lacey normally loved.

But her mind was stuck on pregnancy, and children, and that long-held question of hers she'd never found the answer to. She and her ex-husband had divorced over it, over his desire to have children and her reluctance. If she'd felt like she had no time to raise a child back when she lived in New York City, then how would she ever manage one now when she had a business to run?

At least Chester was enjoying the drive. He was half-hanging out the window of the car, sniffing all the interesting smells of a new, undiscovered part of the country.

Lacey turned onto a small, bumpy dirt path, following it all the way to St. Cyril's Abbey. The monastery was a beautiful dark gray stone structure nestled into the side of a rolling green hill. It was gorgeous, like something from a fairy tale. *Or a horror movie,* Lacey amended. With its mist-obscured turrets and towers jutting up into the overcast sky, and spindly trees like skeletons, the place definitely had a creepy vibe.

Pushing Gina's voice out of her mind, Lacey parked the car and headed toward the imposing wooden door. Chester kept close to her legs as she made her cautious approach and tugged on the rope. A deep bell tolled, making Lacey shudder, then the door was opened and a monk in a long cream-colored gown tied with a rope sash appeared before her.

"Good morning," Lacey said, mustering as much courage as she could. "I'm here for a meeting with Abbot Weeks. I'm a little bit early. I hope that's not a problem."

"That's quite all right," the man said, nodding. "The earlier the better. Please come inside."

He moved away from the door and gestured for her to enter. Lacey peered into the shadows, gulped, and stepped inside. Chester slunk in after her.

The door, it turned out, did not lead into a room or building, rather a courtyard with a covered stone walkway running around the perimeter of an overgrown mass of hedges and statues in the center. Thanks to the tall buildings either side, and the gray day overhead, the courtyard was so dark it may as well have been dusk.

"It's very beautiful here," Lacey commented as she followed the monk around the walkway. He walked so slowly and elegantly he reminded her of a ghost. The fog and old architecture only added to the spooky atmosphere.

"It is. A place of calm and tranquility. St. Cyril's Abbey has been a place of worship since 1087. We've been serving the community for hundreds of years."

"Wow, that's a long time," Lacey said, exchanging a look with Chester. Even though he obviously had no comprehension of the conversation, she still sought him out for comfort.

The monk continued. "As you can see, we're in the middle of some minor repair work." He pointed to a scaffolding structure over to the side, covered in bright orange construction tape. It looked very out of place in the surroundings.

"Is that a bell tower?" Lacey asked, eyeing the tall, narrow tower behind all the scaffolding and tape. Her gaze went all the way to the top, where she could just make out a large bell through the mist.

"It is," the monk replied.

They headed through another doorway on the opposite side of the courtyard, and this time, Lacey found herself in a corridor. The monk guided her to a door with a gold plaque on it that read: *Head Abbot.* He knocked.

"Come in," a voice called.

Lacey recognized it as the same voice she'd heard on the phone last night, male and slightly croaky.

The monk took a step back and gestured for her to enter. He was very polite, but it was also a little disconcerting.

Chester stayed close to her legs as Lacey went inside.

The stone walls were exposed, the floor tiled in the same slate as the courtyard walkway. There was a large mahogany desk in front of her, behind which sat a man in full religious get-up. He was elderly, with a lined face, a large nose, and ears that seemed far too big for his head. He was almost entirely bald, except for a few sporadic tufts of hair. He had a large rosary necklace around his neck with a heavy looking crucifix hanging from it.

The monk who'd led her here did not follow her inside, but instead leaned in and closed the door behind her, shutting her in with the head abbot. Lacey started as the door clicked shut behind her.

"Lacey, please sit," the monk said, standing and gesturing to the wooden chair opposite his desk. "I'm Abbot Weeks. Thank you for coming on such short notice."

Lacey took the seat nervously. "Thank you for inviting me. How can I help?"

"We've been doing some minor construction work," Abbot Weeks explained, his blue eyes regarding her.

"The bell tower," Lacey said. "I saw the scaffolding."

"Yes. That's right. Well, the walls were beginning to crumble, then one opened up, and we found something inside."

Lacey's eyebrows rose as a frisson of excitement went through her. "Something inside?"

She recalled what the monk had told her before, about the abbey being here since 1087. If there was something in the walls since then, it would be one of the oldest items Lacey had ever handled! Any nerves she felt gave way to anticipation. Suddenly, she was chomping at the bit to find out what it was.

"We don't know if it was built into the walls," Abbot Weeks said, leaning out of view down the side of the desk. "Or whether it was hidden there for some reason…"

He straightened up and placed in front of Lacey a wooden box, covered in dirt and debris. There was a latch. Whatever the abbot was talking about was inside the box.

"There's no documentation of work being previously done on the bell tower," Abbot Weeks continued. "Which lends itself to the theory it was put there during the construction. But of course the monastery has been here for hundreds of years, and anything could have happened during that time."

"What is it?" Lacey asked, her eyes fixated on the box, no longer able to hold in her curiosity.

Abbot Weeks nudged the box toward her. "Why don't you open it and take a look?"

Filled with intrigue, Lacey stood. She took hold of the lid of the wooden box with her fingertips and gently opened it. It creaked on its rusted hinges.

And there, inside, lay an old, worn, dirty, ancient scepter.

Lacey gasped.

"What do you think?" Abbot Weeks asked. "Do you think it's worth anything?"

The scepter was not terribly lavish or ornate, though from first inspection it appeared to Lacey that it may well be made of gold. Even if it was not, it would certainly be extremely valuable, simply given the potential age of the thing.

"Absolutely," Lacey said, awestruck. It looked to her like it must've belonged to royalty. "Do you have any history of royal visitors?"

"Oh yes," Abbot Weeks said. "Foreign and domestic. We've even had popes. Do you think it could have belonged to one of them?"

"Whoever owned it was certainly very rich," Lacey theorized.

Abbot Weeks looked thrilled. "The monastery hasn't been doing well financially," he admitted. "The church is considering shutting us down and selling off the ancient building. But if the scepter is of value, then we may well be saved."

"It's certainly of value," Lacey told him. "Though I can't tell you how much precisely. It needs to be properly inspected, cleaned, researched."

"It must be a sign from God," Abbot Weeks continued. "A sign to keep our doors open and continue serving the community. Though we can't offer you anything in the way of payment, we were hoping you'd agree to sell it."

"Me?" Lacey asked. She'd thought they'd just asked her here for advice. She wasn't a trained appraiser. There were surely better people for the task. "I don't know. I'm actually due to get married in a few days, so I'm not sure if taking on such a huge undertaking would be a good idea. I'd need to do a lot of research."

Abbot Weeks looked crestfallen. "It would really help us. We trust you and want to go with a small, respectable business. It would also be for a good cause." He gazed at her with hopeful blue eyes. "A lot of wayward youths would be lost without our services. If we close, they'll suffer too."

Lacey couldn't help but feel for him, and for the troubled youths he was trying to guide. Besides, this was such a unique and interesting opportunity, Lacey would be a fool to turn it down.

"Okay, I'll do it," she said.

"You will?" the Abbot asked, immediately perking up. "How wonderful! I can't tell you how grateful I am." Then he paused. "There is… one small caveat, though."

Lacey felt her eyebrows slowly rise. She didn't like the sound of that one bit.

"And what would that be?" she asked, bracing herself.

"I will need to send a monk with you, to keep an eye on the scepter."

"You'll need to…" Lacey repeated, her voice breathless with astonishment. "A *monk*?" She'd be returning to Wilfordshire with an ancient scepter and a monk as well!

"You won't have to host him," Abbot Weeks quickly explained. "We'll put him up in a local inn. We'd just feel infinitely more comfortable knowing one of our own was there supervising the work. Keeping an eye on things."

He looked at her hopefully. Lacey didn't feel like she had much of a choice. Her interest in the scepter had already been whetted, and her charitable side already appealed to. She wasn't about to turn the work down now—even if that did mean having a monk hanging around the store for the foreseeable future!

"Well, who is the monk?" she asked. "Can I meet him?"

"Of course," Abbot Weeks said, gesturing with his arm to the corner of the room.

Frowning with confusion, Lacey turned in her chair to discover a monk in full regalia standing silently in the corner. Lacey jumped a mile and let out a gasp. Even Chester at her feet whinnied his surprise.

"He's been there the whole time?!" Lacey exclaimed, her hand going to her now pounding heart.

Abbot Weeks smiled. "He has indeed. Brother Benedict is our most recent addition. He joined us through the very same troubled youth program we are hoping the sale of the scepter will save. He has just taken his vow of pacifism, and is now embarking on a prayerful silence. So you can see how he is the perfect man for the job. He's the most invested in the program of any monk here, and he won't cause you any trouble. Indeed, you're unlikely to notice he's even there."

He chuckled, clearly meaning it to be reassuring. But the thought of a silent monk lurking in the corner of her store made Lacey even more disconcerted. Gina would lose her mind.

Lacey turned back in her seat again to face the man. He was young—in his late twenties, she guessed—though his bowl cut and long robe aged him considerably.

"It's nice to meet you," Lacey said, feeling suddenly shy.

In response, Brother Benedict put his hands in prayer position and bowed deeply. There was an elegance in his movements, a slow peacefulness. Something about him immediately put her at ease.

"Brother Benedict's silence will last another ten days," Abbot Weeks explained. "It's an important test for all our new monks. A rite of passage. They must rid themselves of all earthly comforts entirely, so they are open and fully committed to receiving the word of God. He has already completed a three-day water fast, and is now permitted to eat small, plain items such as bread and rice. So you can see he'll be absolutely no bother."

"But I'm not so sure my store is the best place to rid yourself of earthly comforts," Lacey admitted. "It's full of comfortable armchairs, and my staff makes a pot of tea every hour, and my fiancé brings pastries in every day…"

Abbot Weeks cut her off with a kind smile. "I assure you, Brother Benedict will not be tempted. He will be nothing more than a pair of eyes watching over the work. So? Will you accept?"

"I—" Lacey stammered. "Yes. Yes, I'll accept the work."

"Marvelous," Abbot Weeks replied.

He stood and offered his hand to Lacey. She jumped to her feet as well and shook his hand. Then she scooped up the wooden crate containing the scepter and glanced over at Brother Benedict. "Shall we go?" she asked, awkwardly.

The young monk smiled placidly and bowed his head in agreement.

"I'll be in touch as soon as possible," Lacey said to Abbot Weeks as she headed to the door.

"I'm looking forward to it," the head abbot replied.

He showed her out the door and closed it gently behind her.

As Lacey retraced her steps through the monastery courtyard—the wooden crate tucked under one arm and a fully robed, silent monk walking behind her—she was struck by a feeling that she'd just taken on a whole lot more than she'd ever intended.

CHAPTER FOUR

Lacey turned her car into the parking lot of the Lodge, tires crunching on the gravel as she slowed to a crawl and searched for a space.

"My friend runs this inn," she explained to Brother Benedict. "You'll be very comfortable here."

The monk was sitting silently in the passenger seat beside her, a placid expression on his face. He was earning curious looks from Chester, who'd been relegated to the back seat for the duration of the drive.

Lacey parked and killed the engine. "Right. Let's get you checked in, shall we?"

Brother Benedict put his hands in prayer position and bowed.

They exited the vehicle, and Chester ran ahead, springing up the stone steps toward the double glass doors at the top. Lacey had to smile to herself. It almost looked to her as if her dog was running ahead to warn Suzy about the very unusual guest she was about to meet.

Lacey glanced over at Brother Benedict, who did look very out of place now he was out of the monastery. He was carrying a hessian sack over one shoulder, had a blue leather Bible tucked under his arm, and had on a long rosary necklace with a big gold crucifix. Wilfordshire was used to its wild and wacky characters, but Lacey was quite certain it had never seen anything like this.

The pair went through the automatic doors and into the large foyer, with its central stone fountain surrounded by potted plants and gorgeous candelabras. Brother Benedict glanced around as he walked, taking in the beautiful room as he went.

"I designed this place," Lacey told him, proudly. "I used to be an interior design assistant before I took up antiquing."

Brother Benedict gave her his placid smile. Just as he'd done to everything she'd said on the way here. Lacey couldn't help but find it awkward, and a little disconcerting.

They entered the hotel lobby, which was a large, long corridor with dark green wallpaper and various black-and-white photographs on the walls. Lacey immediately heard Chester and Suzy roughhousing. They were very fond of one another.

She guided Brother Benedict up to the large mahogany reception desk, behind which Suzy was playing tug of war with Chester using what appeared to be yesterday's newspaper. Suzy was such a slight young woman, Lacey was actually putting her bet on Chester to win the fight.

"Lacey!" the young brunette exclaimed, as she looked up and fixed her round eyes on her. "There you are." Then her eyebrows rose. "And you brought company?"

"This is Brother Benedict," Lacey said, gesturing to the monk beside her, who dutifully bowed his head. "He's overseeing some antique work I've taken on, on behalf of his monastery."

"How wonderful," Suzy said, smiling at the monk with a pleasant, yet slightly wary expression. "Are you looking for a room?"

"Please," Lacey said, answering for him.

Suzy blinked at her, looking perplexed.

"Brother Benedict is currently in the middle of a holy silence," Lacey quickly explained.

"Righteo," Suzy said. She abandoned her match with Chester and straightened up, smoothing down the creases in her navy blue suit dress. Then she swept her brown hair over her shoulder and out of the way, and began typing into her computer with red-painted fingernails. "Ooh, Brother Benedict, you're in luck. We have just had a cancellation on our best room. Ocean facing. Queen-sized bed. Gorgeous en suite, with a slipper bathtub—"

Her voice trailed away as Brother Benedict began making gentle *stop* gestures with his hands while he shook his head. Suzy looked at Lacey with confusion.

"I think maybe Brother Benedict would be more comfortable in a modest room," Lacey said, remembering what the abbot had told her about his eschewing of all worldly comforts.

The monk smiled and nodded.

"Oh, I see," Suzy replied, tapping away on her computer again. "Would a single room be better? We have one at the back of the building that looks over the lawns instead of the ocean. Or, I guess if you want to go really basic, I could put you up in one of the staff rooms? They only have a bed and closet in them. And no en suite. You'd have to use the staff toilets."

Brother Benedict looked pleased with this suggestion and nodded.

As Suzy typed away, it occurred to Lacey that when Brother Benedict had been glancing about at the foyer, it was not in admiration. Instead, he had probably been thinking about how wasteful and prideful the foyer was. She wondered what he'd think of her store, which was full to the brim with unnecessary trinkets. Perhaps she ought to increase her monthly charity donations to her adopted donkey Alice at the sanctuary…

"Okay, so I've reserved you a room in the staff quarters," Suzy explained. "Do you want breakfast or—"

Brother Benedict was already shaking his head.

"No, of course," Suzy replied with a smile. "You know, I wish all my guests were this easy! Would you like to see your room?"

The monk looked across at Lacey. Of course, his priority was to get to the store and start work on the scepter, as his only purpose at the moment was to oversee that task.

"I think we're just going to head straight to the store," Lacey said.

"No problem," Suzy replied. "Shall I take your bag to your room? Your… Bible?"

Brother Benedict handed the hessian sack to her, his movements exuding calm poise and elegance. Then he patted the Bible under his arm and smiled, as if to say it was staying with him. It was quite astonishing, Lacey realized, just how much communication could take place in silence.

"Well, have a good day, you two," Suzy said, as she slung the sack over her shoulder. She looked at Chester. "And I'll see you soon for a rematch, mister!"

Chester barked.

Lacey headed back out of the Lodge with her dog and monk in tow, and got back into the car. As she turned the ignition, she suddenly remembered the very important errand she needed to do before they got to the store. And that was to go to the pharmacy and purchase a pregnancy test.

"Do you mind if we take a quick detour?" she asked Brother Benedict as she reversed out of the space. "I have an… errand to run."

Brother Benedict gave her an expression of placid acceptance.

Lacey left the Lodge's grounds and headed for the pharmacy, a knot of nervousness in her stomach.

*

Wilfordshire's pharmacy was just as quaint and fancy as the rest of the town's stores. It had an old apothecary feel to it, with wooden shelves and floorboards, and not a hint of clinical white anywhere. Lacey decided to leave brother Benedict in the car, feeling that standing shoulder to shoulder with a monk while buying a pregnancy test would certainly raise a few eyebrows.

She scanned the shelves, looking at the various pregnancy tests available, her mind turning over with worry and apprehension. Who knew there'd be so much choice for a simple test? All the boxes promised things such as the *most reliable*, the *quickest results*, or *UK's most trusted brand!* Lacey grabbed the only one without the overjoyed woman on the front—the last thing she needed was to feel guilty about feeling conflicted rather than joyous.

She approached the counter and took her place behind the tall man currently being served by a female pharmacist in a white coat. But as she halted, she suddenly recognized the man's voice. It was the warm, Kenyan accent of Emmanuel, Tom's assistant at the patisserie.

Of course, Lacey thought. Today was Tom's only morning off, which meant Emmanuel had covered for him and now had the rest of the afternoon off.

Lacey immediately began to backtrack, heading for the shelf to discard the test. If Emmanuel saw what she was buying, she'd have to tell Tom, and she wasn't ready for that yet!

"Oh, ma'am, we're almost done here," the pharmacist said, leaning past Emmanuel and addressing Lacey as she attempted to creep away. "I won't be a minute."

"Lacey?" came Emmanuel's bright, cheery voice. "Is that you?"

Lacey froze in her tracks. It was no use. She'd have to talk to him.

She turned around, hiding the pregnancy test behind her back.

"Emmanuel," she said, forcing out her pleasantries. "How are you today?"

"Wonderful, thank you," he replied, in his ever affable manner. "Except for an ulcer. But this delightful lady tells me that Bonjela will sort me right out."

He grinned at the pharmacist. The woman smiled in return. It was hard not to be instantly charmed by Emmanuel.

"I'll just go fetch your order," the pharmacist told him.

She headed to the back room, leaving Emmanuel and Lacey alone.

"Are you well?" Emmanuel asked as he turned back to face her. "I'm assuming perhaps not, if you're in here?"

"Yes," Lacey said, before remembering she was standing in a pharmacy and needed a cover story. "Actually, er, no, I've just started getting a cough. Probably a cold."

"Oh no! And just before your wedding?" Emmanuel said, sympathetically.

His genuine concern made Lacey feel even worse about lying. But she was between a rock and a hard place here—Tom absolutely had to be the first person she spoke to about this, and so fibbing to Emmanuel was the lesser of two evils by default.

"Hence why I'm here," Lacey replied with a nervous giggle. "Need something extra strength to get me through the day, if it *does* turn out to be a cold. It might just be dust. I've been doing some… cleaning."

Her nervous babbling trailed off as she was luckily saved by the pharmacist's return.

"Here you are, sir," the woman said as she handed a white paper bag across the counter to Emmanuel.

"Thank you, kind lady," Emmanuel said. "You have been most helpful." He turned to Lacey. "I hope your cold passes quickly. If I don't see you before, I'll see you at the wedding." He headed for the exit. "Have a blessed day, all."

And with that, he left, the bell merrily tinkling his exit.

"What a lovely man," the pharmacist murmured. "And how can I help you today?"

Lacey swirled back around, her anxiety increasing in a sudden, big wave. She removed the pregnancy test from behind her back and peered nervously down at it, almost not believing this was really happening. Then she quickly thunked it down on the counter. She may have escaped being spotted by Emmanuel, but it had been an uncomfortably close call, and it made her realize she needed to tell Tom what was going on ASAP before someone else found out and told him on her behalf. Wilfordshire was notorious for its gossipers.

But that also meant finally biting the bullet and having the talk they'd spent their entire relationship skirting around…

As the pharmacist rang up her purchase, Lacey's mind ticked frantically over, going through all her options. If she told Tom but the test ended up coming back false, would it just cause a whole load of worry over nothing? Perhaps she could get this all over and done with without even bothering him…

"Excuse me?" came the pharmacist's voice, breaking through her thoughts.

Lacey flinched. "Sorry. Did you say something?"

The pharmacist gave her a genial smile. "I said that will be fifteen pounds please."

"I must've spaced out," Lacey said as she rummaged in her wallet and handed over the money.

The pharmacist smiled as she counted out her change and handed it back to her. "Maybe you have baby brain!"

Lacey felt her eyebrows immediately draw together. "Baby brain?"

"Oh, you know," the pharmacist continued, conversationally, "sometimes when you're pregnant your brain can get a bit fogged over. A bit spaced out."

Another symptom? Lacey thought, adding it to the nausea and the late period. It was all certainly beginning to build up a picture, one she felt herself becoming increasingly resistant to.

"Heh. Yes. Maybe," Lacey said, feeling dazed.

The pharmacist handed her the little white paper bag across the counter. "Good luck," she said with an encouraging grin.

Lacey took the bag. "Thanks."

She scurried out of the pharmacy, shoving the paper bag as deeply into her purse as it would go.

Then she trotted down the road toward where her car was parked, jumped in the passenger seat, and slung her purse onto the back seat beside Chester.

"Right," she said to Brother Benedict. "Let's go. We've got a scepter to analyze."

As she turned on the ignition, she noticed Brother Benedict in the passenger seat glance over at her bag on the back seat. He was obviously curious about what was inside, and the purpose of Lacey's detour to the pharmacy. But of course, he didn't say a word. For the first time, Lacey was very grateful for his vow of silence. It was a relief to know he wouldn't ask any prying questions.

As she drove the final short distance to the store, Lacey made a decision. She'd take the test just as soon as she got a chance, but whatever the outcome, she'd wait until evening to speak to Tom about it. If it was negative, she could put the whole thing behind her and move on with her life without anyone being any the wiser. If it was positive, well, that would be a whole different kettle of fish. They'd need to have a conversation, a proper one, and neither her antiques store nor his patisserie would be an appropriate location to do it. So whatever the outcome, she'd have her scepter work to keep her nice and busy and occupied. For now she would just put it all out of her mind and get on with her work.

She parked in her usual side alleyway.

"My store is just around the corner," she told Brother Benedict as they exited the vehicle.

She leaned back in and collected her purse and the wooden crate containing the scepter. But as she emerged back onto the sidewalk, she became suddenly aware of a figure approaching. She swirled on the spot.

It was Tom!

CHAPTER FIVE

Lacey immediately felt flustered. Though the pregnancy test was zipped out of sight in her purse, it felt far too close for comfort, almost like she expected Tom to suddenly have X-ray vision and see inside. She awkwardly shifted her purse behind her arm in an attempt to conceal it.

"Lacey," Tom said, beaming as he jogged up to her. "How did your meeting go?"

Lacey was relieved by the line of questioning and grasped hold of it. "Great," she said, sounding perhaps a little too overenthusiastic. She held up the wooden box containing the scepter. "I have a very interesting project!"

"And a monk…" Tom queried, frowning as he looked over to Brother Benedict standing patiently beside the car.

"Oh yes," Lacey chuckled. "And a monk! This is Brother Benedict. He's come to oversee the work. He doesn't speak. Brother Benedict, this is my fiancé, Tom."

"Hi, nice to meet you," Tom said, offering his hand to shake.

Brother Benedict smiled and bowed his head as he took Tom's hand in both of his. It was less of a handshake and more of a gesture of blessing. Tom's gaze darted quickly to Lacey, before Brother Benedict raised his head again and released his hand.

They turned and headed toward the high street together.

"Do you need a hand with that?" Tom asked, looking at Lacey as she fumbled with the big wooden box and her purse.

"No, no," she said, rapidly, moving her purse as far away from him as she could. "I've got it."

As they joined the flow of pedestrians and shoppers on the main street, Lacey couldn't help but feel on edge about the pregnancy test in her purse, and the monk in a gown who was drawing several stares. With her nerves mounting, she mis-stepped and stumbled on a cobblestone. She staggered. Her purse swung off her shoulder and smacked into the wooden crate, which she almost dropped.

"Let me," Tom said, leaping to her rescue.

He motioned for the crate, but Brother Benedict stepped forward and shook his head.

"Oh," Tom said. "I'm not allowed to touch it? I'm sorry." He grabbed Lacey's purse instead.

Lacey managed to right herself and allowed Tom to maneuver the purse off her shoulder. Heat started rising in her cheeks and her heartbeat raced. It was just far too close for comfort!

She clutched the wooden box and quickened her pace, marching as fast as she could. So fast, in fact, Tom had to hop-skip to keep up. Brother Benedict, her monastic escort, floated silently along behind her like some kind of specter.

They reached the store and Lacey drew to an abrupt halt. At last she'd made it to the safety of her store, where she could put these worrisome thoughts out of her mind.

"Here," Tom said, holding up her purse. "Good luck!"

Lacey's heart skipped a beat. "Good luck?" she queried as she grabbed it. "What would I need good luck for?" She nervously giggled.

"With the mysterious job, of course," Tom replied, grinning.

He leaned in to give her a kiss. But just as their lips met, Lacey spotted a very familiar figure walking along the sidewalk on the other side of the road. Dark brown skin. Tall and lithe. It was Emmanuel.

Tom's assistant spotted them right away. "Careful, Tom!" he called jovially across the road. "You don't want to catch Lacey's cold!"

Lacey's stomach plummeted. She'd been so close! Now she'd have to fib again. And this time in the presence of a man of God!

Tom drew back from her and gazed at her with concern. "Are you getting sick?" he asked, worried, placing the back of his hand on her forehead as if feeling for a fever.

"Maybe," Lacey said rapidly, swiping his hand away awkwardly. "I don't know. It's just a headache. Probably stress. Don't worry. Anyway…" She looked at Brother Benedict. "I don't want to leave our guest standing out here in the cold. I'll see you later!" She turned from Tom and opened the door, making the bell tinkle loudly. "Bye!" She hurried inside before Tom even had a chance to reply.

Perhaps keeping the results of her pregnancy test from him all day wasn't prudent after all. If she saw two pink lines, it would be far too much of a burden to bear. She'd have to wait until evening to take the test.

"You're alive!" Gina exclaimed, before Lacey was even halfway inside her store.

Chester nudged past her legs and raced over to greet Boudica.

Lacey stepped fully inside. "I told you nothing bad would happen."

But as she moved aside to allow Brother Benedict to enter in behind her, Gina jumped a mile.

"A ghost!" Gina cried.

"No, Gina," Lacey said. "This is Brother Benedict. Abbot Weeks sent him to oversee the antique work they'd like me to do for them."

Gina stared at the monk nervously as he followed Lacey inside the store, his ever-placid expression plastered to his face.

"Are you sure?" she queried. "He's … floating."

Brother Benedict smiled at that.

"He's just very calm and tranquil," Lacey replied. "Maybe you should take a leaf out of his book." She addressed Brother Benedict. "Gina is our resident stress pot."

Again, he smiled.

"Lacey," Gina said. "I really think he might be a ghost. Why isn't he saying anything?"

Brother Benedict actually laughed aloud at that. Presumably expressions of joy were not forbidden during his ten-day silent prayer. Lacey was just glad he wasn't offended by Gina's rude questions, or the way she was speaking about him as if he wasn't actually present.

"He's in the middle of a prayerful silence," Lacey explained. "Ten days. And he'll be spending most of his time in the back room with me while I work on this." She gestured to the wooden box under her arm.

"What is it?" Gina said.

Lacey was about to explain when Brother Benedict gently laid a hand on her arm to stop her. She remembered Abbot Weeks's instructions to keep the work a secret. She'd assumed it would be all right to explain it to her colleague, but evidently not.

"Sorry," she said to Gina. "It's top secret."

Gina pouted. She hated to be left out of the loop. "Well, fine. But don't you go getting all obsessed with whatever it is and forget about your wedding. I know what you're like. There's still the itinerary to go through, and we have to make confirmation calls to all the vendors."

Lacey sighed. None of Gina's tasks actually had to happen. It was all just extra work Gina had made up to fuss and stress over. And *Lacey* was supposed to be the obsessive one?

"Gina, please relax," Lacey said. "Everything will be fine."

Gina narrowed her eyes. "That monk's rubbing off on you. Since when were you so Zen about everything?"

Lacey gave her shoulder a small shrug and smiled at the calming presence of Brother Benedict. "I guess he is rubbing off on me," she agreed. She gestured to the box under her arm. "Shall we?"

Brother Benedict nodded, and they headed off to the small back office to begin work.

Chester decided to come with Lacey, rather than guard the main store. He must have felt she needed supervising from the strange robed man. Which amused Lacey, since the strange robed man was supervising the scepter. It was like a very bizarre set of Russian dolls.

"Please take a seat," Lacey said to Brother Benedict, as she lowered herself in the office swivel chair and placed the wooden box on her desk.

Brother Benedict looked at the spare chair, then shook his head, before moving to stand in the corner of the room just as he had done back in Abbot Weeks's office. Clearly, the cheap plastic office chair was still too comfortable for his tastes, and despite how disconcerting it felt having him lurking in the corner, Lacey wasn't going to question it.

She got to work, opening up the lid of the box and marveling once again at the scepter inside. Then she put on medical gloves and fetched her loupe.

As she peered at the scepter through the magnifying glass of the loupe, she noticed a phrase inscribed on it. But it was so dirty, she could only make out some of the letters. It didn't seem to be in English. Latin perhaps.

She began to carefully clean the scepter, working in gentle, minute movements to brush away the loose layers of dirt and dust. But even after her surface-level cleaning, the inscription was no clearer.

Lacey didn't feel comfortable doing a deeper clean just yet. She didn't want to damage or scratch the scepter in the process.

"Brother Benedict," she said to the monk poised like a statue in the corner. "I'm going to need to contact a specialist. I know Abbot Weeks wants this to be a secret, but there's no way I can do this without support. Should I call him first to discuss it, or can you approve it?"

Brother Benedict smiled and nodded, and Lacey took that to mean he was okay with her reaching out to a specialist.

She swirled in her chair to her computer and went online, tapping at her keyboard as she scoured the internet for some local religious scholars. She found a forum for an archaeological society, and found a scholar in the vicinity named Crispin Noble. Beneath an icon of the local Exeter College emblem, his bio line read: *Professor of*

Archeology, Latin Geek, Proud Hufflepuff. She couldn't help but chuckle at the Harry Potter reference.

There were several icons next to the emblem: quotes marks, an envelope, an ear with a line through. She guessed the envelope would be the way to DM him, and clicked it. A bubble popped up on the screen with an accompanying noise.

"*Dear Professor Noble,"* she typed, *"I'm writing with regards to a scepter, possibly dating back to 1087. There appears to be a Latin inscription on it. I would love to arrange a meeting with you, perhaps here at my antiques store on Wilfordshire High Street? Please let me know asap, as this work is quite urgent."*

She hit send and the bubble disappeared with a *ding.* Then she swirled in her chair to face Brother Benedict.

"All done," she said as she spun. "I've contacted a specialist. Let's hope it's not too long before they get back to me. I know you're eager for this work to be done as quickly as possible."

But when she stopped turning to face Brother Benedict in the corner, she was surprised to see Chester had fallen asleep *on* his feet. Yet the monk had not moved a muscle or made a sound.

"I'm so sorry!" Lacey exclaimed, hopping up from her chair. "Chester, boy, come on now, off the nice man's feet."

Her canine companion grumbled as, pink-cheeked, she guided him to the space beneath her desk.

*

Knock-knock-knock.

Lacey turned to face her office door.

"Come in!" she called.

As the door creaked open, she suddenly realized it would be Gina trying to snoop at the scepter, and quickly covered it with a sheet.

"It's home time," Gina said, poking her head around the door. Her gaze roved over to the monk in the corner. She visibly shuddered.

Surprised, Lacey looked over to the clock on the wall. It was already half past five. "Oh! Is that the time? I got totally distracted by my work."

"Are you coming?" Gina asked.

"Actually," Lacey said, thinking of the pregnancy test in her bag that she'd promised she'd take this evening, and suddenly wanting to avoid it, "there's a bit more I want to get done here first." She looked at Brother Benedict. "Would you like Gina to drive you to the Lodge?"

Behind the door, Gina's eyes widened, and she started vigorously shaking her head. Clearly she did not want to give a lift to the monk she suspected was in fact a ghost.

Brother Benedict opened his hands toward the lumpy sheet concealing the scepter, and smiled serenely. Lacey took that to mean that as long as she was working on the scepter, he was happy to remain present.

"I think we're both going to stay here actually," she said to Gina. "I can drive Brother Benedict to the Lodge once I'm finished."

By the expression on Gina's face, this suggestion was even worse than her giving him a lift home herself.

"How long are you planning on staying?" Gina asked with concern. "It's already dark."

"Gina," Lacey said with gentle warning. "Everything is fine. You head home, and I'll see you tomorrow."

Gina wrung her hands together, then finally nodded. "Okay, fine. I'll leave you two to it." She looked at Chester. "Goodnight, boy. No biting!" She chuckled as she looked up at Brother Benedict. "He might look nice but he has a very vicious side. I've seen him take down a grown man double your size. And he's impossible to outrun."

Brother Benedict's eyes widened.

"Gina!" Lacey cried. "That's enough now. He's harmless," she assured Brother Benedict.

"Oh yes, harmless," Gina replied leadingly. "Just as long as you're a decent person with good intentions. Chester can sniff out a bad egg better than anyone. Just thought our friend here would like to know." And with that, she turned on her heel and walked away.

"I'm so sorry about her," Lacey said, shaking her head. "She's under a lot of stress."

Brother Benedict smiled. He appeared unfazed.

Lacey turned back to the scepter and removed the sheet, eagerly getting back to work.

CHAPTER SIX

Lacey felt a gentle pressure on her back, a warm, almost comforting feeling. Then she suddenly jerked to sitting as her awareness returned to her. She was in her office, working on the scepter, and had just nodded to sleep in front of her guest! The warm pressure on her back had been Brother Benedict's hand, gently bringing her back to the land of wakefulness.

She coughed awkwardly into her fist and let out a nervous laugh. "I should probably take that as a sign that it's time to finish for the day and lock up." She quickly wiped the back of her hand across her mouth in case of drool. Luckily, that was one embarrassment she didn't need to endure. Whether she'd snored during her brief moment of sleep she would never know—though if Tom's teasing was true, then she certainly had. Heat warmed her cheeks.

Brother Benedict gave her a kind smile, as if telling her there was no need for embarrassment.

"Let me show you where the safe is," Lacey said, rapidly, snatching up the crate.

As she led Brother Benedict into the back room, Lacey couldn't help but analyze what had just happened. It wasn't like her to fall asleep at her desk. Could the fatigue be from stress, or was it another symptom of pregnancy? Her stomach flipped at what felt like yet another unwelcome puzzle piece falling into place.

She crouched down at the safe, turning the dials of the lock and popping it open. Then she opened the door and placed the scepter inside, nestling it next to a beautiful sapphire necklace hanging from a hook. The necklace was part of Iris Archer's estate, and was Lacey's most precious keepsake, since it came from her very first auctioneering job.

Lacey shut the thick door to the steel safe and put the padlock back on, turning the combination, as she always did, to *0000.*

"Are you happy with that?" she asked Brother Benedict as she straightened up. "With keeping the scepter in a locked safe, inside a locked store?"

Brother Benedict smiled his agreement.

Lacey led Brother Benedict and Chester out of the store and into the now frigid, dark evening. Lacey locked up the store, being extra cautious under the ever-watchful eyes of Brother Benedict, and then they walked the short distance to the side street where her car was parked. They got inside, and Lacey slung her purse into the backseat beside Chester, who was once again looking thoroughly displeased to be in the back seat rather than his usual spot up front.

Lacey turned the ignition and pulled onto the road, driving up the cobblestone street.

"My family is flying in tomorrow," she told Brother Benedict as she turned at the pub onto the promenade road and joined the row of cars heading for the hillsides. "And I need to pick them up from the station. So I won't be doing any work on the scepter until after lunch. I'm not sure what you want to do in that time."

Brother Benedict put his hands into prayer position.

"You'll pray?" Lacey translated.

He nodded.

"All morning?"

He nodded again.

"Cool," Lacey replied.

She had a lot of respect for Brother Benedict. Her life always felt so busy and stressful and anxiety-ridden, and she had to admit that at least half of it was of her own making. She'd come to Wilfordshire in the first place seeking out a quieter and more simple life, only to have slipped back into her old busy ways. Brother Benedict, on the other hand, was so calm. He needed for nothing. Nothing fazed him.

In fact, his calming presence was starting to make her feel less stressed herself. Maybe having him here during the stressful family reunion would work in her favor. At the very least, it would give her parents something to talk about other than just character assassinations…

She reached the Lodge and Brother Benedict bowed his head as he exited the car.

"See you tomorrow afternoon," Lacey called as he closed the door gently behind him.

As she watched the robed figure heading up the steps of the Lodge, Chester immediately jumped from the back seat into his vacated spot, his tail smacking Lacey in the face as he went.

"Hey!" Lacey exclaimed, spitting out fur. "You were supposed to be guarding my purse. It was a very important job."

Chester harrumphed as he settled into his favorite seat.

Lacey looked at the purse lying on the back seat. Inside was the pregnancy test. And now, she realized nervously, the time had finally come for her to go home and take it.

*

Lacey turned into the driveway of Crag Cottage, her headlamps illuminating the front of her stone cottage momentarily, before she cut them out and darkness fell.

As the engine hissed to silence, Lacey took a moment to pause. The time had come to take the pregnancy test, and she was full of conflicting emotions about it. But it was time to be brave and find out once and for all.

She leaned over and took her purse from the back seat, cradling it nervously in her arms, then got out of the car.

"Lacey!" came Gina's sudden voice.

With a flutter of panic, Lacey quickly checked her purse was zipped up securely. It was. Then she looked over to see Gina jogging across the lawns waving an arm over her head. Her friend was wearing her pink dressing gown and matching fluffy slippers, and she looked perturbed to say the least.

"Gina, is everything okay?" Lacey said, immediately worrying. "What's happened? You look like you were in bed."

"I was!" Gina cried melodramatically. "But I couldn't sleep. I was worried about you. I thought maybe the monk had turned into a homicidal maniac!"

Lacey rolled her eyes affectionately and gave her friend's fluffy pink arm a squeeze. "No, dear. I just ended up working late." She remembered the embarrassing moment she'd dropped off to sleep at her desk in front of Brother Benedict. "I lost track of time. Very absorbing research," she added, hurriedly.

Gina didn't look pleased. She put her hands on her hips. "Young lady, you do make me fret. Promise me you won't do that again, at least not while our spooky guest is with us."

"I promise," Lacey said. "Although you must stop calling Brother Benedict spooky. It's not very polite. He's a real human with real feelings. And I'm actually growing very fond of him."

"Probably because he doesn't speak," Gina exclaimed. "I'm sure you'd be very fond of me too if I wasn't always telling you off."

"I'm already very fond of you!" Lacey told her, warmly. "You know it very well."

But Gina was not to be reassured. She got like this sometimes. Up on her high horse, and too committed to her rightful indignation to come back down.

Lacey watched as she turned with a harrumph and marched back across the grass. Then the pink fluffy blob disappeared through the gap in the hedgerows and out of sight.

Lacey sighed. She loved Gina to death, as a friend, neighbor, confidante, and colleague, but just not so much as a surrogate mom. She got enough fussy over-parenting from her own mother all the way in New York City; the last thing she needed was a second one right on her doorstep.

"Come on, Chester," Lacey said as she went up the garden path.

Her dog followed her as she retrieved the Rapunzel key from her purse and opened the front door. Together, they stepped inside the cottage, and Lacey flicked on the lights to make it cozy and comforting.

Her eyes immediately went to the staircase ahead, to the spot where Tom had witnessed her in her wedding dress. Had it been a bad omen? In a moment she was going to ascend that staircase for the bathroom and take the pregnancy test—would it tell her something she did not want to know? Set her life on a course she had not intended? There was only one way to find out.

Lacey headed upstairs, her purse clutched in her arms as if it contained precious cargo, and entered the bathroom. She caught her own reflection in the mirror, seeing the anxiety in her brown eyes and purple sleep-deprived bags beneath them.

She took a deep breath and removed the pregnancy test, holding the box in her hands. Such a small little thing, wielding so much power.

Just then, her phone started to ring. She checked the screen to see it was her mom calling. Lacey knew better than to let her mom's call go unanswered, so she put the test down and took the call instead.

"Hi, Mom," she said into her cell.

Shirley's voice sounded in her ear, immediately launching into conversation with little pleasantries. "Darling, I'm calling to let you know we're at the airport. Now, the flight gets us into Heathrow at eight AM local time, then we're catching the train to Exeter. The timing didn't work out as well as I'd hoped, because there's actually a train *at* eight but we'll obviously miss that, and then the next one isn't until eight thirty. Which means we'll have to hang around in the airport, although Naomi seems to think it will take us that long to get our bags back and Frankie wants to do some plane spotting!"

She chuckled. Lacey narrowed her eyes. Where was her mother's monologue going?

"Okay," she said aloud. "So I'll come pick you up from the train station at nine."

"Oh right, that's why I was calling you actually. We won't need picking up from Exeter. We're going to take a cab to Wilfordshire."

"Are you sure?" Lacey asked. "It's a half-hour journey. It will be quite pricey."

"It's fine. Frankie requested it. He's very into transport at the moment. Vehicles and such. He's very excited about experiencing driving on the left-hand side, and has a million questions about it. We'd like him to have all his car talk out of his system when we meet up with you, so we can actually have a proper catch-up, and Naomi and I have decided it would be better for everyone if the person whose ear he talks off about it is an outsider. We'll both have already had hours of listening to him talk about airplanes on the flight, and another hour of him talking about trains."

Lacey smiled as she thought of her ginger-haired nephew and his obsessions.

"Okay, as long you're sure," she said.

"We're sure," Shirley replied. "Hopefully we'll both be able to get a nap in the back seats while he's up front chatting away!"

Lacey chuckled. "Okay. Well, I'm looking forward to seeing you all." She made the calculation in her head. "At nine thirty-ish."

"You too, darling."

"Have a good flight."

And with that, the call cut out.

Silence fell around Lacey once again.

Lacey's eyes went to the pregnancy test, only this time she thought about Frankie, and what it might be like to have her own son, full of curiosity and enthusiasm. She and Frankie had a great bond and she thoroughly enjoyed the time she spent with him. If being a mother was anything like being an aunt, then what was it that she was so afraid of?

As she plucked up the courage to take the test, Lacey found herself pondering over where her deep-seated fear of motherhood really came from. She'd always thought she just wasn't that fond of children. She was too career-orientated. Much more of a dog person. But her love of

Frankie had forced her to consider there was more to it—another, deeper layer.

She set the test on the side and read the instructions. It would take two minutes to develop. Two minutes! A maddening amount of time! If the result was positive she'd see two pink lines. If it was negative, she'd see just one.

Lacey paced across the bathroom floor, chewing her nails. Her mind turned over again and again as she ruminated on all her anxiety over the chances of it being positive. Did that fear stem from her own childhood? Her parents had been so wrapped up in their own issues during her childhood that she and Naomi had been often overlooked. Was it less about having a child per se, and more about an irrational fear that she and Tom would suddenly turn into her parents, and repeat those same destructive patterns? Surely, if that was where it came from, it was irrational. She was nothing like Shirley, and Tom was nothing like Frank, and the way they behaved with one another—loving, supportive, respectful—couldn't be further from the way her parents had acted during their marriage.

Just then, her phone rang again and she jumped a mile. She rushed back to the sink where she'd left it, to see Tom's name flashing up at her.

Her heart skipped a beat. Should she tell him what she was doing? What if this was all a false alarm and she worried him over nothing? Or what if she told him and his reaction was completely mismatched to hers, that rather than worried and conflicted he was thrilled? What if it all became like it had been with David?

With a nervous tremor in her hand, Lacey answered the call.

"Hello fiancée," came Tom's bright, cheery voice in her ear.

"T—Tom, hi," she said, her mind racing. Why did she feel like a naughty child who'd been caught red-handed?

"Gina tells me you were working late," Tom said, oblivious to the pregnancy test currently developing on the side of the sink, a single solid pink line beginning to come into existence. "Is that a good idea in your state?"

"My state?" Lacey echoed, her heart rate spiking. "What do you mean by that?"

"Because of the headache," he said. "Or cold. Or whatever it is that's wrong with you."

Oh, Lacey thought. *That.*

"It's fine, it's passed now. I don't think I'm coming down with anything." She eyed the test warily.

"Thank goodness," Tom said, merrily. "I'd hate for you to be sick on our wedding day. Anyway, I figured you'd be too tired to cook tonight, so I took it upon myself to bake a meat pie. Want me to come over?"

"That's very sweet," Lacey said, her eyes glued to the pregnancy test as the pink color strengthened. "But I'd like a quiet evening alone before my family descends."

Tom chuckled. "Fair enough. It's going to be chaos! They are booked in at the Lodge this time, right?"

"Yes," Lacey said. "Thankfully."

She'd learned her lesson about sharing accommodations with her family from their disastrous trip to Dover in the summer. Not that her family's arrival was the total reason she wanted to be alone. The other, of course, was the pregnancy test. Whatever outcome Lacey got, she knew she wanted to sit with it by herself for a while, to process her own feelings before telling Tom. It sure seemed to be taking its sweet time to develop!

"Okay, darling," Tom said. "All the more pie for me, in that case. I'll see you tomorrow. Love you."

"Love you too," Lacey replied.

She ended the call and grabbed the test, holding it up to her eye line. The first pink line was now completely solid in color, but in the space beside it, something was starting to change.

CHAPTER SEVEN

Was it a second pink line? A very faint one? It was barely visible. More of a thin, gray line than a thick pink one.

She grabbed the instructions again. Pregnancy meant two solid pink lines. In the picture they were chunky pink things. But her test was showing one pink line and one thin gray line!

“Dammit!” Lacey exclaimed.

The test was inconclusive.

After all that stress and worry, she was no closer to finding her answer. She’d need to take another one, but of course after having worked late, the pharmacy was now closed. And worse, when would she find the time to squeeze in an extra trip to the pharmacy? Her family was arriving early, then there was lunch, and then in the evening the dreaded family meal to reintroduce her father to everyone. With all that on her plate, and her family hovering around her, Lacey had no idea how she was going to find either the time or the privacy to take a second test.

With a defeated sigh, Lacey dropped her head into her hands. Tomorrow was going to be difficult anyway. Now, with all this hanging over her head, it was going to be doubly hard. Maybe Gina was right about the omen after all.

*

Lacey headed to the Lodge early the next morning. Since she didn’t need to pick up her family from the airport anymore, there was no reason not to get on with the scepter work. Besides, she was really appreciating the distraction. She’d struggled to sleep last night, worrying about the inconclusive pregnancy test, and how she was ever going to find the chance to take another one now that her family was coming. She’d prefer to see a doctor, really; she didn’t trust the flimsy over-the-counter tests anymore and she certainly didn’t want to get one of the other brands, the ones with the delighted women on the boxes.

She pulled into the parking lot, and she and Chester headed inside the Lodge. Suzy was at the desk, looking half-asleep with a coffee clutched in her hand.

"Morning, Lacey," she said with a yawn. "You're here to collect your monk, I presume."

Lacey chuckled. "I am indeed."

"He's in the grounds," Suzy said. "The night staff said he was up at the crack of dawn, and he's been pacing around the garden ever since. I'm glad all the guests are still asleep. I think they'd get a fright if they spotted a robed monk walking laps around the garden. It's like something out of a horror movie."

"I'll go fetch him," Lacey said with a chuckle.

She left Chester with Suzy for their tug-of-war rematch, and headed into the gardens.

It was a gray, overcast day, with a hint of moisture in the air. The grass was dewy and fresh. Lacey scanned the gardens and spotted Brother Benedict walking a slow lap past one of the flower beds Gina had planted when she was contracted to landscape the lawns. They were bare at the moment, due to the frost, but come spring they'd be alive with color.

"Brother Benedict!" Lacey called, as she trotted down the red brick steps toward him.

The monk looked up and smiled.

Lacey drew to a halt beside him, feeling the damp from the grass at the hem of her pant leg.

"There's been a change of plans," she said, her breath coiling on the cool air. "My family is getting a taxi to town instead. So, if you don't mind me interrupting your prayers, would you like to come to the store and get back to work on the scepter?"

The monk smiled genially and bowed his head in agreement.

They headed back inside the warm, cozy inn together, and along the corridor to the reception desk. Chester had completely destroyed the newspaper.

"He won," Suzy said, shrugging in defeat. "What can I say? He's a true champion."

Chester barked happily.

Lacey, Brother Benedict, and Chester left the Lodge and climbed into the car. With all her stresses racing through her head, Lacey wasn't much in the mood to make one-sided small talk with a monk. But luckily for her, Brother Benedict didn't need to be entertained. He was actually a very calming presence. Being with someone while she was feeling stressed but with no responsibilities or expectations was actually hugely comforting.

She reached the high street, which was starting to open up for the day, and parked in her preferred spot down the side street. Then she led her robed companion to the store.

As she began to open up the shutters, she heard someone calling her name.

"Lacey? Oh Lacey!" It was Taryn.

Great, Lacey thought wryly. *Little Miss Blabbermouth. Just what I need.*

She turned and smiled at Taryn, who was tottering along the high street in her heels, balancing a cardboard tray with two takeout cups from the Coffee Nook in one hand and clutching a bulging brown paper pastry bag in the other. Lacey frowned. She knew Taryn didn't eat pastries—or breakfast, or anything, come to think of it—and wondered whether the boutique owner was expecting guests.

"Morning, Taryn," she said, barely able to fake her politeness this morning.

"This is for you!" Taryn exclaimed, beaming. She thrust the paper bag at Lacey's chest, surprising her.

"Oof," Lacey said, clutching it. It was warm. "What is this?"

"Breakfast," Taryn replied.

Half-curious, half-skeptical, Lacey opened up the bag. The smell of delicious sugar and buttery pastry wafted out at her, making her salivate. She peered inside, expecting a prank and to find out Taryn had put something awful in there like bugs. But no, it was indeed full of pastries. And they looked utterly delicious.

Bemused, Lacey glanced back up at Taryn. "You bought me breakfast? Why?"

"Well, your family are flying in today, aren't they?" Taryn replied with a single-shouldered shrug. "And I know how demanding they can be. I thought you'd need something to keep your energy up, since you're always working so hard and forgetting to eat properly."

Me forgetting to eat?! Lacey thought, looking at Taryn's rake-thin frame.

"That's very kind of you," she said aloud.

Even though she knew Taryn was probably only doing it to get an invite to the wedding, she was genuinely touched by the gesture. Besides, Chester wasn't even growling at Taryn anymore, a habit he'd had the whole time Lacey had known him. If he could warm to her, then Lacey certainly could as well.

"Did you want to come in and share them?" Lacey asked.

Taryn shook her head. "No, no. Not for me." She looked at the monk standing beside Lacey. "You can share them with this …relative of yours?"

"Oh!" Lacey exclaimed, amused by the idea of having a distant monk cousin. "This is Brother Benedict from St. Cyril's Abbey. He's helping me with some work."

"Sounds exciting," Taryn said. She curtseyed to the monk. "It's very nice to meet you."

"He doesn't speak," Lacey explained.

Taryn let out a delighted gasp. "He sounds like my kind of man!"

Lacey rolled her eyes and unlocked the door. Taryn, it seemed, would flirt with anyone, be it Lacey's elderly father or, in this case, a man who'd taken a vow of celibacy.

The lock yielded and Lacey gestured Chester and Brother Benedict inside. Lacey followed, pausing in the open doorway to look at Taryn, still standing in the street.

"Well, thanks again for this," Lacey said. "It was really kind of you."

"You're very welcome," Taryn said, not moving a muscle.

Lacey realized what was going on. She wanted the invite. Right here, right now. Well, Lacey wasn't about to give it to her.

"I'd better get on with my work," Lacey added, taking hold of the door and starting to close it.

"Right," Taryn replied. But still she did not move.

"Got a lot to be getting on with," Lacey continued.

Taryn just wasn't getting the hint. She left Lacey no choice but to begin to slowly shut the door on her.

"Oh, and Lacey," Taryn called when there was just an inch of space left, "do let me know if you'd like to do anything this week. I have a completely clear schedule! It could be anything, morning or night. Even a group thing would be fine!"

"I'll let you know," Lacey said, finally closing the door.

It shut with a click and Lacey let out a sigh. Then she turned, only to discover Brother Benedict was standing there, watching her with an extremely amused expression on his face.

"She's fishing for an invite to my wedding," Lacey explained.

He raised his brows in what appeared to be a questioning manner. He probably wanted to know why she wasn't inviting her.

"It's complicated," Lacey mumbled. "Come on, let's get to work."

They headed into the back office. Lacey turned on her computer to see whether Crispin Noble, the archaeology specialist from Exeter College, had emailed her back. But before she even had a chance to log in, she heard the loud sound of Gina coming in through the main door.

"Cooey! Lacey?" she cried. "Where are you?"

Lacey gave Brother Benedict a look. "Please excuse me one moment," she said.

She headed onto the shop floor to see what Gina wanted, only to discover her friend was not alone. There was a man with her.

"Look who I just bumped into," Gina said.

Lacey gasped.

CHAPTER EIGHT

"DAD?!" Lacey cried, staring at her father standing on the welcome mat of the store. He was dressed in his farmer's garb, a big waterproof jacket, mud-streaked pants, and dirty wellies with manure and hay stuck to the bottoms. Through the window, his old cattle truck was parked badly in the street.

"Hello, sweetheart," Frank said.

Lacey hurried to her father, arms wide, and they embraced.

But as she moved out of his embrace, Lacey suddenly panicked. He wasn't supposed to be here until evening. Her mom, sister, and Frankie were due to arrive in half an hour and this was not how she wanted the family reunion to go down. She had to get rid of him, and quick!

"What are you doing here?" she asked.

"I wanted to surprise you," Frank said.

"You surprised me, all right," Lacey replied, breathlessly. "I didn't think you were driving up until the meal this evening."

"I thought it would be nice to have breakfast together first," Frank said. His voice dropped. "Just the two of us."

Lacey could tell from his expression he was anxious about the family reunion dinner later, and she couldn't blame him. Her mom and sister had given him quite the frosty reception during their awkward speakerphone conversation. Though things had been tense between Lacey and Frank initially, at least he had the comfort of knowing she'd attempted to find him, that despite all the conflicting emotions over his abandonment of her as a child all those years ago, she must have forgiven him in some way or she would never have gone to such lengths to find him. But the others? They would have happily seen out the rest of their days without ever seeing him again. The thought must weigh on him terribly, Lacey thought.

But as bad as she felt for her father in his time of insecurity, she absolutely did not want them all bumping into one another. She needed to think of an excuse to get rid of him.

"I'm really sorry, Dad," she said, pointing to the paper bag of pastries she'd left on the counter. "I've already had breakfast, courtesy of Taryn. And I have a ton of work to be doing this morning."

"Lacey decided to take on a mystery antiquing project," Gina interjected, explaining the situation with more than a hint of disapproval. "Right before her wedding! And right after Tom accidentally saw her in her dress." She shook her head and tutted.

Frank frowned with confusion. But Lacey didn't want to get into it. In fact, she didn't have *time* to get into it. The clock was ticking away. Her family was due any minute.

"I could take you for breakfast though," Gina continued.

That just wouldn't do. Lacey wanted Frank out of Wilfordshire entirely. Not only did she not want her dad and mom accidentally bumping into one another in town, she didn't even want them accidentally spotting one another! The plan was to introduce everyone properly over dinner, in a controlled, comfortable, and extremely chaperoned situation.

"Actually, Gina," Lacey said quickly with a hinting tone, "I really need you to help me with something this morning."

"Let me guess," Gina said, folding her arms. "It's something to do with the monk?" She looked at Frank and added with disdain, "This extra work is for a monastery."

Lacey tensed. Gina was clearly not picking up on the hint, and the more she brought up about the monastery work, the more questions she was raising, and the longer it would take for her to get rid of her dad. She simply didn't have time to explain the whole scepter situation right now!

"Right, fine, you guys go for breakfast," she said, quickly amending her plans. If she couldn't get her dad out of Wilfordshire entirely, at least having Gina the chatterbox occupy him for an hour with all her superstitions over the monastery situation would be the next best thing. "Have a long breakfast, though. And somewhere special, not on the high street. And wherever you go, don't sit by any windows! Because of… UV."

They both looked confused as she ushered them out the door and into the distinctly overcast drizzly English winter day, where the last thing anyone needed to worry about was getting sun damage.

As soon as the door shut behind them, Lacey glanced at the clock. Ten past nine. That felt like a close call! But Gina and Frank should be settled in somewhere and out of sight within the next twenty minutes. As long as they followed her instructions and took a long breakfast, Lacey should have enough time to get her mom, sister, and nephew in and back out again before they returned.

She was about to return to her work when the door opened behind her and the bell went. Of course, with Gina out of the store for the foreseeable future, she'd now have to juggle all the customers alone. Just what she needed, when she had so many other things to do!

She turned as a man with brown hair and a beige plaid shirt beneath a blue waterproof winter jacket walked in. He scuffed his shiny black brogues on the welcome mat and looked up at Lacey poised in the middle of the shop floor.

"Hello," he said, jovially. "I'm here from the archaeological society."

"Oh!" Lacey exclaimed with surprise. "You must be Crispin Noble." She'd not had a chance to check her emails yet that morning, having been interrupted by Gina and her father. But it was quite obvious from the man's attire that he was a professorial type. "I didn't realize you were planning on dropping by," she continued. "And so soon. I must say, that's very quick. I only emailed you yesterday."

"Well, when someone finds an ancient scepter with a Latin inscription, it's really impossible for someone like me to resist!" he exclaimed.

"Come with me, I'll show you," Lacey said. "Although, I must warn you in advance, I am a Gryffindor."

She chuckled. But her Harry Potter reference didn't elicit quite the response she was expecting from Crispin Noble. Instead of laughing along, he merely blinked. Perhaps he took being a Hufflepuff very seriously…

"Chester," Lacey called over to her dog. "Can you please be on duty?"

Chester trotted to the door and took up his sentry pose.

"He's well trained," Crispin commented, as he followed Lacey under the arch.

"Oh yes, he's very obedient," Lacey said over her shoulder. "My very own Hedwig."

Once again, her Harry Potter reference fell completely flat. She wondered whether Professor Noble had actually written his bio on the archaeological website after all. Maybe he had naughty children who'd gone in there and changed it for him on his behalf for fun!

She headed into the office, where Brother Benedict was standing silently in the corner.

"This is Brother Benedict," she said to Crispin.

Crispin visibly started when he realized there was a robed monk standing there, completely still and in utter silence. A hand fluttered to his chest.

"He's overseeing the work with the scepter," Lacey explained, quickly. She was so used to Brother Benedict now she'd forgotten just how disconcerting his presence was to begin with. "He doesn't speak. Brother Benedict, this is Professor Noble from the archaeological society."

"Nice to meet you," Crispin said hesitantly. He held a hand out to Brother Benedict, looking uncertain about whether this was the correct way to greet a monk. Brother Benedict took the hand in both of his and bowed. It was halfway between a handshake and something altogether more pious, and Crispin smiled nervously in response.

"The scepter is locked in the safe," Lacey explained. "If you'd like to come with me."

She led the two men out of the office and into the back room where the big steel safe was. Then she put in the combination and pulled open the thick steel door, before removing the wooden crate containing the scepter. She laid it carefully on the table at the side and lifted off the wooden lid, revealing the half cleaned golden scepter lying inside.

"Oh gosh," Crispin said in awe. "Oh goodness me."

He tiptoed closer and peered down at the scepter with widening eyes. It almost seemed to Lacey that he knew exactly what he was looking at.

"Do you recognize it?" she asked, feeling the first flutters of excitement inside of her.

"I do," Crispin replied, sounding almost mesmerized. "I know exactly what you have here. That's more than a relic—it's a treasure."

Lacey heart skipped a beat. *Treasure?* That sounded very mysterious! Images of pirates with stolen bounty stashed away in the walls of the monastery popped into her mind. She glanced at Brother Benedict to see whether he was as excited as she was, but he appeared to be as placid as always.

She turned back to the gawking Crispin.

"So you know what it is?" she pressed, eager for more. "You know who it belonged to?"

"I do," Crispin replied, almost breathless with wonder. "And I'd be very happy to tell you…"

The anticipation made Lacey's heart race even faster. She felt like she was on tenterhooks, and held her breath in expectation.

Crispin straightened up and looked her straight in the eyes. "…But I'll only tell you what I know if you agree to split the profits from its sale with me."

Lacey felt herself deflate like a balloon. Her eyebrows drew in together. "What?"

Professor Noble's demeanor suddenly changed. Gone was the wide-eyed, awestruck, affable professor, and in its place instead was a greedy Golem.

"Fifty-fifty split," he said firmly.

"I'm not selling it," Lacey said abruptly. "At least not for profit. It belongs to St. Cyril's Abbey." She pointed to Brother Benedict. "The proceeds are going to them so they can continue their community work. My involvement here is charitable."

Crispin huffed and folded his arms. "That's a shame. I thought you wanted my expertise. But clearly not."

Lacey was shocked. Affronted. "I do want your expertise, but there's no money involved."

"So you expect me to help you for free?" Crispin replied with a tone of utter contempt.

Lacey's mouth fell open. She could not quite believe how childish this man's behavior was! He was acting less like a professor and more like a pupil! First he was humorless about her Harry Potter references, and now he was being stubborn about sharing his wisdom. What an awful man. He'd come across as so friendly and sweet from his profile at the archaeological society forum, but clearly judging someone from how they presented themselves on the internet was a fool's errand.

Lacey opened her mouth to argue back, when she was cut off by the sound of Chester barking. He was alerting her to someone entering the store. She looked at Brother Benedict.

"Could you please supervise our *friend* here?" she asked, putting emphasis on her sarcastic choice of endearment. "I have to attend to a customer."

Brother Benedict nodded.

Lacey turned on her heel and marched away, still fuming about the encounter with the awful Professor Crispin Noble.

When she made it to the shop floor, she noticed a man waiting at the counter, bundled up in a gray duffle coat with a yellow and black striped scarf. He smiled at her as she slid in behind the counter.

"Lacey?" he said, holding out his hand to shake. "I'm Professor Crispin Noble from Exeter College. I'm here about your message."

Lacey's mouth dropped open. Suddenly it twigged that the yellow and black stripy scarf were the colors of Hufflepuff! *This* was Professor Crispin Noble. But then … who was that in her back office?!

CHAPTER NINE

Lacey blinked with astonishment at the man standing at her counter. "I—I'm sorry. *You're* Crispin Noble?"

"That's right," he said, his expression becoming disconcerted as he took in Lacey's stunned response. "Is everything okay? I sent you a message about dropping by today, but I can leave if it's not a good time."

"No, it's..." Lacey shook her head. "It's just that... you're already here!"

Professor Noble's eyebrows drew together. But before Lacey had a chance to say more, a sudden movement came from behind.

Her heart flew into her mouth. She swirled around to see the imposter now standing in the archway behind her. She felt suddenly very afraid. Who was this strange man pretending to be someone he was not? How had he even found her?

"Who are you?" Lacey demanded, her voice quivering with fear.

But rather than looking menacing or dangerous, the imposter's face turned beet red. His eyes were wide as he regarded the man standing at the counter. He looked like less of a threat and more like a naughty child caught with their hand in the cookie jar.

"WHO ARE YOU?" Lacey demanded again. This time the fear in her voice was replaced with fury. How dare this stranger come here and try to dupe her? He had a lot to answer for!

"I—I—" he floundered. "I'm just a treasure hunter. That's all."

He darted the rest of the way through the arch and hurried past Lacey and the real Crispin Noble, beelining for the store door. Chester tracked the shady figure as he went, tail wagging with curiosity, looking very eager for Lacey to give him the command to take the man down. And she was very tempted. Something untoward was definitely going on here. But the fake Crispin's evident embarrassment made her feel it was not criminal, and didn't warrant unleashing her guard dog upon.

"A treasure hunter?" she called after him as he scarpered across the floorboards. "What does that mean? How did you find me?"

He reached the door and hauled it open, making the bell jangle noisily. "Consider my offer," he said hurriedly. "Fifty-fifty. It's a good one." And with that, he made a very undignified exit, earning himself a disapproving *yap* from Chester.

As the dust settled on the strange encounter, Lacey leaned both her hands on the counter to steady herself from the shock. Her heart was racing. Her mind turning. What had just happened?

The real Crispin Noble turned back from the door where he'd been watching the whole scene unfold. He frowned, looking utterly bemused. "I'm sorry, but what on earth is going on here?"

"I wish I knew," Lacey replied. "That man," she stammered, pointing at the door, "was pretending to be you!"

Professor Noble's eyebrows rose slowly. "He was… *pretending to be me?* But why? I must say that's a first."

Lacey was utterly confounded by it all. "I can only assume it was so he could see the scepter. But now I think about it, he only ever said he was from the archaeological society. I just presumed it was you, since you were the one I emailed, and I suppose he just went along with it for whatever reason. Come to think of it, I emailed *you* specifically. So how the heck did some random treasure hunter know how to find me?"

"Ah," Professor Noble said. "Actually, you didn't email me. You put your message on the society's forum. It's a public forum."

Lacey gasped. "You mean to say anyone can read it?"

"All and sundry, I'm afraid," Professor Noble said.

"I said to come to my antiques store on Wilfordshire High Street," Lacey said with a groan. Her heart plummeted as the gravity of her mistake set in. "This is the only antiques store on Wilfordshire High Street!"

The real Professor Noble nodded. "That's how I found you. I fear it will now be very easy for any fraudster to find you. Just a few quick search terms will lead any opportunist in this direction."

"Oh no," Lacey said, shaking her head with frustration.

She felt terrible about her mistake. Now only would everyone now know about the scepter in her store, but the secret she'd promised to keep for Abbot Weeks was out of the bag. The head abbot had strictly forbidden her from talking about it even to Gina, but now anyone with an interest in archaeology could find it!

"I don't understand how the message went public," Lacey continued. "I thought by pressing the envelope icon I was emailing you privately."

"I can see how that would seem confusing," Professor Noble said, looking genuinely bad for her. "The website is very old. It's been operating since the nineties. The infrastructure hasn't changed since then. It can be less than counterintuitive to navigate. Here are my credentials, so you can be assured I am who I say I am." He fumbled in his jacket and fished out a lanyard. He showed it to her. It was his Exeter College ID.

"I should've known he was an imposter from the get-go," Lacey said. "He barely reacted when I forewarned him I'm a Gryffindor."

Professor Noble's eyes lit up. "Oh!" he exclaimed, letting out a nervous giggle. He waggled the end of his scarf. "And I a Hufflepuff. Perhaps our fake friend was a Slytherin? Posing as a different person would be quite a Slytherin thing to do."

Lacey couldn't help but laugh in reply. "I suspect you're right about that!"

With the tension now broken, Lacey's emotions over being duped began to fade. It was still a frustrating situation, but she was more interested now in getting on with the scepter work, rather than picking over the deception with a fine-tooth comb.

"I'd better show you the object that's caused all this fuss," she said to the real Professor Noble, "now that we can be sure you're who you say you are."

"Thank you," the real Crispin Noble said. "I'm quite excited."

"This way, then," she replied, beckoning him to follow her. "And just a heads-up, I have a monk guarding it. He doesn't speak. I figured it was best to tell you now, since you've already had one nasty surprise today."

Crispin smiled as he followed after her. "That's most considerate of you."

They headed into the back room. The box with the scepter was still laid out open on the table, with the ever-watchful eye of Brother Benedict keeping it safe. Lacey could tell from the look in his eyes that he was baffled by what had just transpired. It almost looked like he was curious enough about it to break his prayerful silence, but he held back and simply nodded at Lacey and the different man walking in beside her, who was in fact the real Crispin Noble.

"Here," Lacey announced, gesturing to the scepter. "Feast your eyes on that."

Professor Noble paced closer, adjusting his spectacles as he went. "Hmm."

He began inspecting it from all angles, quirking his head this way and that in a manner that reminded her of a bird.

"Hmm," he said again, leaning in so close his face was right in the crate.

Lacey couldn't help but feel a little disconcerted. His reaction was very different from how the treasure hunter had behaved, and *hmm* wasn't telling her very much at all. Perhaps she'd been mistaken in thinking the scepter was valuable?

With growing nerves, she glanced back at Brother Benedict. He seemed even more nervous than she was. He was watching Crispin Noble with a look of anxious expectation in his eyes.

"Well," Crispin said, straightening up.

"What do you think?" Lacey asked immediately.

"Well," he said again.

The anticipation was killing her. His reaction was so muted, so different from the treasure hunter's, Lacey couldn't help but fear that the scepter wasn't a piece of treasure at all, and that the treasure hunter had just been faking his reaction in an attempt to make it seem more alluring, and to nudge her toward selling it for profit.

"Well?" Lacey prompted, wringing her hands with increasing anxiety.

"I'm not sure," Crispin said finally, in a moment of complete and utter letdown. "May I take a photo? I will have to do some research. It will help to have a photograph to draw back on."

Lacey chewed her lip. It seemed the "secret" scepter was becoming less and less so with every moment that passed. She looked at Brother Benedict for guidance. He nodded.

"Go for it," she said to Crispin, though she was far from thrilled about it.

As the professor began to snap several photographs from different angles, Lacey felt a sudden wave of nausea overcome her. With a spike of panic, she thought again of the pregnancy scare she'd been trying so hard to ignore.

"I'm sorry not to be much help," Crispin said as he worked. "But I'm sure with some research I'll be able to find some answers for you."

Lacey swallowed, the sick feeling wavering inside of her. "Anything you can do will be appreciated," she squeaked.

As he continued taking photos, Lacey tried to focus her mind away from the wave of nausea and back to the moment. But it was no good. The more she tried to ignore it, the stronger it seemed to become, and now her salivary glands were getting in on the action to, flooding her mouth with fluid as if in preparation for hurling.

Suddenly, she felt a hand on her arm. She looked over to see Brother Benedict looking at her with concern. Though she'd been discreet and tried to hide her nausea, the perceptive monk had sensed something was wrong. But without having to say out loud what it was that was bothering her, and knowing she was no longer alone in her discomfort, Lacey suddenly felt a calmness overcome her. The sick feeling subsided.

"I think that's enough," Professor Noble said, straightening up and returning his cell to his pocket. "Leave this with me. I'm on the case."

Now fully recovered from her fit of sickness, Lacey smiled at Crispin. "How long do you think your research will take?"

"I can't say," Professor Noble replied. "But I promise to keep you in the loop every step of the way. I suspect I won't have anything until the morning at the earliest."

Lacey led him back out to the shop floor and escorted him to the door. "Okay, thank you, Professor. You've been very helpful."

She shook the man's hand, and he headed out into the street.

She was about to close the door after him when she heard voices coming from the distance. It sounded like a commotion had broken out farther up the road. By the accents of the people involved, Lacey deduced it was some kind of ruckus between tourists. American tourists…

Suddenly, she realized she recognized the voices. It was her Mom, Naomi, and Frankie. But they were early!

Immediately panicked, Lacey peered out the door and up the street, wondering how on earth they'd managed to make trouble when they'd literally only just arrived. But when her eyes found the three of them clustered farther up the road her stomach dropped into her toes. They were not alone. There were two other figures with them. One was Gina. The other … was Frank.

CHAPTER TEN

Lacey's chest sank as her eyes homed in on the sight of her family halfway along the high street, arguing with one another. This was exactly the scenario she'd been hoping to avoid.

In a panic, she raced out of her store and ran along the cobblestone street toward where her family had clustered together. The closer she got, the more of the scene she digested and the worse she felt.

Shirley, it seemed, was the aggressor. She was squaring up to Frank—despite him having well over a foot of height on her—and was wagging her pointer finger in his face. Her floral traveling case was lying in the gutter as if she'd literally flung it aside to free up her hands. Why she needed her hands free, Lacey dreaded to think.

A small audience of onlookers had gathered and were watching the scene unfold with equal parts fascination and concern. Lacey's toes curled. She hated being the center of attention at the best of times; she couldn't think of a worse circumstance to have so many eyes on her than the one she was about to rush into.

The devil on her shoulder told her to turn back around and let her parents sort out their own problems—they were both adults, after all—but when she spotted her sister openly weeping into her hands while being comforted by her gingernut nephew she had to accept the only person who could resolve this situation was her. This was her responsibility. She had no choice but to throw herself into the fire.

"Mom! Dad!" she shouted as she drew up to them and halted beside a stunned-looking Gina. "Please calm down! Let's talk about this!"

But neither of her parents seemed to even notice her. They were so wrapped up in their own emotions it was as if they had forgotten the world existed outside of them.

"You're a disgrace!" Shirley was busy screaming at Frank. "Call yourself a man? What kind of man walks out on his children? His wife?"

Frank meanwhile just stood there, taking the berating and giving Shirley nothing in return. This evidently riled her further.

"Well?" she demanded, her face going a deeper shade of red. "What have you got to say for yourself?"

The audience was murmuring to one another, clearly thoroughly entertained by the drama unfolding on the streets of their quaint little town. Lacey felt a pit open up in her stomach. All those prying eyes. All those whispers and stares. And this whole ruckus was her fault in the first place. She was the one who'd tracked Frank down and asked him to walk her down the aisle.

"Mom!" Lacey tried again, pleadingly. "Please calm down!"

But her words fell on deaf ears.

Gina turned to her, a stunned look on her face. "Lacey, I'm so sorry," she exclaimed, having to raise her voice over the din. "The second Frank spotted them out the window he went running."

"I told you to take him off the high street!" Lacey cried, raising her own voice which was at a risk of being entirely drowned out by Shirley. "And to sit away from the windows!"

"I know, I know," Gina said, shaking her head apologetically. "I'm sorry."

There was no point dwelling on that now. What was done was done, and the only thing left to do was find a solution.

Feeling flustered, Lacey turned back to her family. She quickly assessed the situation and decided that Frankie was her best bet. How telling that out of the three of them, the eight-year-old was the most sensible, the one most easily reasoned with.

She hurried over to her ginger-haired nephew, forcing a smile onto her face.

"Frankie!" she exclaimed, trying to look happy and in control for his sake.

He saw her and grinned. "Aunty Lacey!"

He made motions to embrace her, but then looked at his weeping mother and clearly thought better of it. Lacey ruffled his ginger curls instead.

"I'm so happy to see you," she told him.

"You too," Frankie said. "Only, I don't understand why Grandma is shouting at that man and why Mom is crying."

"Well," Lacey said, taking a deep breath. How to condense thirty years of hurt into a soundbite suitable for the ears of an eight-year-old? "That man is actually your grandpa. And your grandma is shouting at him because sometimes when people love each other a lot they can get really hurt when the other person does something mean to them."

"Oh," Frankie said, looking like he was taking it all in. "So is he mean?"

Lacey shook her head. “No. He’s a good man. But he did a mean thing, once upon a time, and Grandma hasn’t forgiven him yet. Neither has your mom.” She looked over at Naomi, who was still covering her eyes with her hands, but was now peeking out through her fingers at Lacey.

“Hey sis,” Naomi snuffled.

“Hey,” Lacey said. She opened her arms for a hug. Naomi hesitated, then folded into them.

The two sisters held one another tightly as the sound of their mother unleashing thirty years of hurt reverberated around them.

“Thirty years!” she shouted. “Thirty years, Frank! Without a word. I thought you were DEAD!”

The audience of onlookers was making Lacey’s toes curl. She needed to get away from all these prying eyes.

She moved out of Naomi’s embrace and looked into her sister’s brown, tear-filled eyes. “How about you and Frankie go to the store?” she suggested gently. “It’s just up there on the left. Gina can go with you. You can say hi to Chester and Boudica. Have a cup of tea.” She cast a wary glance at her parents. “While I deal with this.”

Naomi sniffed her tears and nodded. She took hold of the handle of her case in one hand and Frankie’s hand in the other, then tipped her chin up.

“Gina?” Lacey said. “Can you take Naomi and Frankie to the store and make them a snack and tea? I’m sure they’re famished after their journey.”

Gina looked instantly relieved to have some way of making amends with Lacey.

“Of course, right this way!” she exclaimed, beckoning Naomi and Frankie to follow her. “I told the dogs you were coming. They’re both very excited.”

Lacey watched them begin to walk to the store then turned back to her quarreling parents. Stressed, embarrassed, and feeling totally caught in the middle of an impossible situation, Lacey took a tentative step closer.

“Mom! Dad!” she exclaimed, forcing herself to stand right int the middle of them.

At last, they finally noticed her presence and stopped shouting. And it had only taken her wedging herself literally in front of their faces to achieve it!

Shirley blinked at Lacey as if coming out of a trance. “Oh. Hello.”

"Hi," Lacey said through a tight jaw. She turned to Frank, as the more reasonable of the pair. "Dad, I really need you to go somewhere else right now, okay?"

"What? Why?" her father asked. "We're meeting in a few hours anyway."

"Then you only need to kill a few hours, don't you?" Lacey replied, tersely.

Frank sighed. "This is silly. I just want to speak to them."

"Silly?" Shirley began to squawk. "Did you really just have the audacity to call my pain *silly?!*"

"As you can see, now is not a good time," Lacey said to Frank, raising her voice to be heard over Shirley's cries. "Or place!" She gestured to the watching crowd.

Frank looked about himself. It was if he hadn't even realized they were drawing the attention of everyone on the high street, and was now surprised to see the gathered crowd. But it didn't seem to embarrass him in the same way it did Lacey. Perhaps, she wondered, that was because he didn't live here and wouldn't have to walk past them every day for the rest of his life!

"Please, Dad," she pleaded. "They're all jet lagged. They've been traveling for hours. Emotions are running high. There's a reason why I planned the dinner as a reunion, rather than the middle of the street."

She couldn't help but feel annoyed that her carefully considered reunion plans had been for nothing. What a waste of effort. She shouldn't have even bothered trying. Maybe she should just lock the two of them in the back office to hash it out. They'd wear themselves out eventually. Brother Benedict could officiate…

But no. Lacey reminded herself this was for Naomi. Her fragile sister simply couldn't cope with the drama in the same way Lacey could.

Lacey found her resolve once again. She slung her arm around Frank's shoulder and guided him away from the screeching Shirley.

"Why don't you go for a cliff hike?" she suggested. "You love the Wilfordshire cliffs so much, and I can lend you Chester if you want someone to keep you company. It's just for a few hours, until they're settled in."

Frank considered her suggestion for a moment. Then, reluctantly, he said, "Fine. I'll go for a hike. But I don't need Chester, I'm perfectly capable of walking on my own." He paused and gave her a kiss on the cheek. As he drew back, his gaze went over her shoulder at Shirley, who was scowling so deeply her entire face seemed to be all frown. "Good luck with her," he muttered, ruefully.

"I heard that!" Shirly screamed, before launching once more into her rant. "And you've got some nerve! I'm only like this because of YOU! Thirty years of worry, not to mention ten godawful wasted years of marriage!"

"Save it for dinner!" Frank shouted back.

Shirley scoffed.

Lacey sighed and gave her father a gentle but firm push in the opposite direction, steering him away from Shirley. The one thing that was worse than the pair of them nose-to-nose in a screaming match was the pair of them several feet apart in a screaming match.

"Dad," Lacey urged. "Go!"

Finally, Frank relented. With a stroppy huff, he turned on his heel and marched away, shoulders hunched, hands shoved deeply into his pockets.

Well, that could've gone better, Lacey thought as she watched him strop away. *But at least no fists had flown.*

It pained her to see her father that way. It was not a side of him she'd seen before, or at least, not since getting back in touch. She may well have witnessed this behavior before as a child. It was quite far from the jolly man in the laundry room who seemed able to take Shirley's sniping in his stride. And she certainly didn't care for it.

Feeling like she was carrying the weight of the world on her shoulders, Lacey turned back to her mother. She'd picked up her floral carry-on case from the gutter and was holding it tightly in her arms like it was a punching bag. Lacey approached and prized it from her hands, then looped her arm through hers.

"Shall we go to the store and talk?" she said, forcing out a calmness she did not feel.

Shirley snorted from her nose. She was still watching Frank as he slunk away along the cobblestones. "Fine," she replied.

Red-faced and embarrassed, Lacey guided her away from the crowd. She already felt weary and the visit had barely even begun. This was exactly the opposite of how she'd wanted the trip to start. Things with her mom could be difficult at the best of times, and now the whole trip had started off on the wrong foot.

But she couldn't help but feel sympathy for her mother and for what her father had put her through all those years ago. And she felt very protective of her as she marched along with her head held high against the staring passersby.

As they reached the store, Lacey cast a glance across to the patisserie. Luckily it appeared to be crowded inside, which meant Tom had not witnessed the horrible fight. Lacey was glad for the small mercy.

She led the way inside her store.

Frankie, Naomi, and Gina were sitting on the vintage couches with a pot of tea and an impressive spread of sandwiches and vegetable sticks on the coffee table before them—even more impressive considering the short amount of time Gina had had to cobble it together. Clearly, she was going all out to make it up to Lacey.

Frankie was halfway through chewing a carrot stick slathered in hummus when he spotted Lacey and Shirley entering. He shoved the rest in his mouth and jumped up. "Yay! Aunty Lacey's here!" he said through his mouthful. He hurried up to her and hugged her.

Despite the anguish Lacey had felt moments earlier, it was all worth it to see her nephew and get a hug from him. Even if he did have sticky fingers…

"How's everyone doing?" she asked, glancing at Naomi.

Her sister seemed to have stopped crying now, though her face was still red and blotchy.

Lacey worried the most about her. It just seemed to be shock after shock when it came to their father, and she wasn't sure how well her fragile younger sister was coping.

"Maybe you guys should go straight to the Lodge?" Lacey suggested. "I'm friends with the manager, and I know she'd be happy to let you check in early. You all look exhausted after the journey. Perhaps a nap would help? Then we can meet for lunch just like we planned."

Shirley folded her arms. "You're trying to get rid of us."

Lacey tensed. Great. They really were off to a flying start, weren't they?

"No," she said, gently. "I'm trying to give you all a bit of time and space to decompress. It was never my intention for you to bump into Dad like that, and it must've been an awful shock for you all. So a rest might be a good idea. For all of us."

Shirley pouted. She hated to be outsmarted by her daughter, or even admit that she was right. But she clearly understood Lacey was talking sense. She snatched up a sandwich from the platter. "Fine. But I'm taking these with me."

"Help yourself," Lacey said. "Let me just get my keys."

She headed over to the counter where her spare car keys were kept beside the register. As she went, Gina leapt up from the couch and scurried after her.

"Lacey," she said, grasping her arm. "I'm really sorry about everything."

"Why didn't you just do what I asked in the first place?" Lacey asked her with an exasperated sigh.

"I didn't understand," Gina told her. "You didn't make it clear."

"I was dropping hints left, right, and center," Lacey said, making it to the counter and heading behind. "I thought the whole point of a maid of honor was to make things run smoothly." She snatched up her car keys. "I'm going to drop my family off at the Lodge, and ask Finnbar to come and help you here."

Gina looked affronted. "I don't need help! I can handle the store on my own."

"This isn't up for debate," Lacey said, playing her rarely used "Boss" card. "There's too much going on here for one person to manage. I'm expecting a scholar to get in touch about the scepter. We have Brother Benedict to look after. And obviously we have the usual shop stuff to do. You're stressed over the wedding, so let's have Finnbar come in and ease some of the workload."

"He has a paper to write. He won't want to."

"He always has a paper to write," Lacey countered. "And I know he wants the money."

Gina looked like she was about to quibble again, but thought better of it. "Fine," she muttered.

"Great. I'll see you soon," Lacey replied. She got her cell phone out of her pocket with her spare hand so she could call Finnbar on the walk to the car. "Don't do anything crazy while I'm gone. Okay?"

"Yes, yes," Gina said dismissively.

At least there was a monk there to stop her from doing anything too stupid. He seemed to have a sensible head screwed onto his shoulders.

Lacey whistled for Chester, then whisked her family up, sandwiches and all, and ushered them to the door. Hopefully, with her Dad hiking the cliffs of Wilfordshire and her family napping in the Lodge, she'd be able to get an hour or two breather to collect her thoughts and work on the scepter. Perhaps the worst was now over, and with a bit of luck, things would be smooth sailing from here on out. But on the other hand, Lacey knew luck had never really been on her side.

CHAPTER ELEVEN

"Hey, Gina," Lacey said as she emerged from her office several hours later. "Will you be able to mind the store for five minutes?"

She'd spent the last hours after dropping her family off at the Lodge therapeutically cleaning the scepter, in blissful silence under the quiet presence of Brother Benedict and a snoring Chester. Gina had left her alone ever since she'd gotten back—avoiding her, no doubt, because she was still in a bad mood from her earlier dressing down, and annoyed that Finnbar had agreed to come over for the afternoon shift while Lacey was on her lunch date with her mom, sister, and nephew. He'd not arrived yet, but Lacey wanted to take the only opportunity she'd get today to purchase a second pregnancy test for later.

Gina looked over at her and pouted. "Why?" she asked. "Where are you going?"

Lacey felt her cheeks warm. Now was definitely not the right time to tell her friend about her pregnancy scare. "I just have an errand to run. It will take me five minutes. Finnbar's on his way. Brother Benedict is praying in the office… or sleeping. It's hard to tell sometimes. So, can I trust you to take care of things for five minutes?"

"Can you trust me?" Gina replied, grumpily. "You don't need to ask."

Lacey rolled her eyes. She could really do without Gina's attitude on top of everything else.

"Chester," she called. "Let's go."

Her dog came trotting. On this day when it seemed like everyone was annoyed at her, it was nice to have someone's unflagging support.

Lacey headed out of the store with Chester in tow, and walked along the cobblestone street to the pharmacy. Before heading inside this time, Lacey peeped through the windows to make sure there was no one she knew inside. The coast was clear, so she went in.

The bell overhead tinkled as she beelined for the shelf of pregnancy tests. Her eyes scanned the array of different brands once again. Since the last one had been so inconclusive and irritating, she decided to go with a different brand, even if that did mean having to look at a very happy, smiling model. She picked the test deemed "most trusted brand," and headed to the counter.

The same pharmacist in the white coat was on duty again today. "In need of a second opinion, I see," she commented as she rang up the pregnancy test.

"The last one was inconclusive," Lacey explained. "One pink line. One gray one."

"Doesn't sound inconclusive to me," the woman said. "Sounds positive." She grinned and held out her hand. "Fifteen pounds, please."

Lacey did not move. The second the pharmacist said positive, she'd frozen to the spot with shock.

"Sorry, did you say…"

"…Positive?" the pharmacist said. "Yup. Two lines usually means pregnant, even if the test was only able to pick up a very weak signal."

"But…" Lacey stammered. "But then why would the box show two fat pink lines as pregnant! It was very clear. Mine was one pink line and a thin, barely visible gray line!"

"Maybe you were dehydrated. That can do it. Or did you pee on it properly?"

"I know how to pee on a stick!" Lacey exclaimed.

The pharmacist shrugged. "Well, I guess you'll know for sure once you've used this brand. It's considered much more reliable. That last one you got is notorious for dud results."

Lacey narrowed her eyes. "Then why do you sell it?"

"Not all women want to be pregnant," she replied simply. She pointed at the overjoyed model. "The packaging upsets them."

Lacey ground her teeth. But what could she do? There was no time to book a doctor's appointment and have an actual, reliable test done. And now the pharmacist had strongly hinted that the first test was positive, there was no way she'd be able to put it off until after the wedding.

Frustrated with the whole situation, Lacey reached into her purse, only to find her wallet was not inside.

"Dammit!" she cried, realizing she must have left it at the store. "I forgot my wallet."

The pharmacist gave her a knowing look. "See. Baby brain," she said with a smirk.

"Heh," Lacey replied. "I, er, I'll just have to go and fetch it. Can you hold on a minute?"

"Of course," the pharmacist said.

She set the test to the side, but it was still well within eye-shot of anyone passing by. And since Wilfordshire was full of nosy gossipers, Lacey didn't like the thought of someone seeing her leave the pharmacy and the test on the counter and put two and two together.

"Could you maybe put it out of sight?" she asked the pharmacist, feeling a little foolish.

A flicker of confusion appeared on the pharmacist's brow, before she smiled politely. "Of course."

She moved the pregnancy test to a more covert position, and Lacey scurried out with Chester and raced back to the store.

As soon as she opened the door of her store, she was hit by a blast of cold wind. Lacey immediately knew what that meant; Gina was out in the garden, probably tending to her winter squashes, and had left the patio door wide open, creating a wind tunnel. The store felt like an ice block.

Lacey shivered as she hurried past a snoozing Boudica and into the back office to search for her wallet. Brother Benedict was standing in his usual corner, eyes closed, perfectly still and silent. Lacey had started to suspect he'd mastered the art of sleeping standing up.

She rummaged through her things, searching for her wallet and not finding it.

"Where did I put that damn thing?" she mused allowed.

The pharmacist's comments replayed in her mind. Baby brain. She quickly pushed them away.

"I'll try the back room."

She headed inside and started searching through the room. But as she searched, something peculiar caught her eye. The safe didn't look quite right.

Abandoning her task, Lacey inched closer, peering at the big bulky lock. Then she gasped. The combination on the lock, which she always turned to *0000* once she had locked it, was showing a different series of numbers.

A jolt of worry went through Lacey. She thought back, trying to recall whether she had forgotten to set it after she'd last used it, but the number on the lock wasn't the actual combination, it was a completely random series, almost as if someone had been…

Lacey gasped.

Someone had been in the store, and they'd tried to get inside the safe!

The worry in Lacey's chest turned to full-blown panic. She let go of the lock, noticing now what appeared to be scuff marks all around the seal of the steel safe door. Someone had attempted to pry their way in! She'd been gone for barely five minutes, but there was clear evidence that someone with ill intentions had been inside.

"Gina!" Lacey cried, suddenly worried for her friend. What if the person had harmed her? Kidnapped her?

Lacey's mind turned into a frantic stream of fantastical ruminations as she hurried out the back room and through the auction room to the patio doors standing wide open. Chester raced along behind her, looking at her with an expression of curiosity and concern. They raced into the garden side by side.

Breathing raggedly, Lacey glanced around searching for any sign of Gina.

Suddenly, she spotted movement coming from the greenhouse. She gasped, thinking immediately of an intruder. But then she recognized the frizzy gray hair, the Wellington boots, the big flowing skirt. It was Gina, pottering about in the green house without a care in the world. Her friend was entirely unharmed, busily tending to her plants, oblivious to the sheer panic she'd just caused Lacey.

Knowing she was now safe, Lacey stopped worrying, and switched immediately to anger mode. She marched into the greenhouse.

"Gina!" she snapped.

The older woman swirled, looking startled. "That was quick." She frowned. "Is everything okay?"

"What's going on?" Lacey demanded.

Gina gestured to the terracotta pot in front of her. "I'm tending to my squashes."

"I mean with the store!" Lacey cried. She put her hands on her hips. "You left it unmanned! Unlocked!"

"Boudica was in charge," Gina replied.

Fury burned Lacey's cheeks. "Boudica? The world's sleepiest dog? Well, guess what. She didn't do a very good job of it."

"What are you talking about?" Gina asked with a frown.

"Someone's been in the back room," Lacey revealed. "They've had a go at getting into the safe."

Gina gasped. But a second later she shook her head with disbelief, and waved a dismissive hand. "You must be imagining things. It's impossible. Boo would've barked. And what about Ben?"

"Ben?"

"Brother Benedict," Gina corrected. "He's been here the whole time, meditating away silently in your office. Don't you think he would've heard something?"

"Look, I'm not making it up," Lacey contested. "Come with me. I'll show you."

She led Gina back inside the store, crossing through the auction room and dipping her head in through the door of her office. The monk was standing in his usual corner, eyes closed, expression serene.

"Brother Benedict?" Lacey said, gently.

His eyes opened. He looked at her with a placid smile.

"I think you might want to come with me. This pertains to the scepter."

The monk put his hands in prayer position and bowed. He followed her out of the room, his robes swishing as he went.

Lacey led everyone over to the safe.

"See the marks?" she asked, gesturing to the scuffs and dents around the door.

Gina and Brother Benedict leaned in, both squinting as they peered closely at the safe.

"They've been there for months," Gina finally said, drawing back. "Remember when that man tried to steal the jewels from Penrose Manor? He was the one who made the dents."

Lacey hesitated. Maybe she was going off on the wrong tangent here? But no. What about the combination?

"The combination has been changed," she explained. "I always set it to *0000.* At the very least someone's been trying to guess it."

Gina and Brother Benedict both looked blank.

Lacey huffed. "You guys really heard nothing?" she asked.

They both shook their heads.

Maybe Lacey was really going mad…?

Just then, a sudden sound came from behind. Lacey and Gina jumped out of their skin. So too did Brother Benedict, who was usually poised.

They all spun to the door. Finnbar was standing there.

"Is everything okay?" he asked, taking one look at their panicked faces.

"Not really," Lacey said. "I think someone's been in the store, trying to break into the safe."

Finnbar's face dropped. His hazel eyes registered fear. It was the last thing an anxiety-prone person like Finnbar wanted to hear.

"There's no thief," Gina refuted. "Lacey's going mad. She thinks someone managed to get in, in the five minutes she was out and I was in the greenhouse. But me and Ben didn't hear a thing, and neither did Boo."

"Who's Ben?" Finnbar asked.

"The monk," Gina said.

"The monk?"

"The monk!" Gina cried, losing her patience. "The monk! The bloody monk standing behind you!"

Finnbar glanced over his shoulder at Brother Benedict. "Oh," he said, surprised. "Hello." Then he looked back at the women and whispered, "Why is there a monk here?"

"Long story," Lacey said. "The short version is he's helping oversee some work I'm doing for St. Cyril's. It's regarding the item inside the safe."

"Which has been tampered with," Finnbar said, piecing it all together.

"Exactly. The combination has been changed," Lacey explained.

Finnbar's eyes immediately widened. Clearly he agreed with Lacey in thinking the change of combination was a red flag. Lacey felt vindicated as he hurried toward the safe and grabbed the padlock. It helped to know that at least one person had their head screwed on right.

"She's right," he said, turning over his shoulder to face the others. "Someone's definitely tried to guess the combination." He ran his fingers over the scuffs and dents of the door seam. "Looks like they used a crowbar."

Lacey immediately shot Gina a look. "See."

Gina pouted and folded her arms. "Well. I honestly don't understand. There are valuables all over the place. Why go for the safe?"

"Because the person who did it wanted what's inside," Lacey said.

Her mind went straight to the sketchy treasure hunter. Had he done this? It certainly seemed possible. He was immoral enough to impersonate someone else, and seemed money-hungry and greedy.

"What's inside?" Finnbar asked. He was still trying to get up to speed. "I know the jewels from Penrose Manor are in there. What else?"

"It's a scep—" Lacey began, before Brother Benedict stepped forward and rested a hand on her arm. She managed to stop herself just in time. "—I can't say. It's a secret. The item in the safe belongs to St. Cyril's."

Finnbar frowned. "Why is it secret?"

"Just part of the conditions," Lacey said. "The head abbot asked me to keep it secret. Only Brother Benedict and myself, and a trusted scholar know what's inside." Then her chest dropped. "And a con man…" She looked at Brother Benedict. "I really think it was that treasure hunter from before. The one who pretended to be Professor Noble. He saw me open the safe. He knows what we have inside. Do you think it was him too?"

Brother Benedict regarded her with consideration. His eyes registered interest but ultimately he seemed unwilling to cast the first stone. Lacey had a gut feeling but maybe Brother Benedict was right not to rush to judgment.

Finnbar looked back and forth from Lacey to the monk and back again. "Is he…telepathic or something?"

Gina groaned. "They've been doing this all day. Talking with their eyes."

"Sorry," Lacey said, snapping back to the moment.

"Why don't we check the cameras?" Finnbar suggested. "The ones Frank installed? If someone was here, they'll have been picked up on them."

Everyone paused. It was a very pragmatic suggestion.

They all headed to the main shop floor to check the surveillance footage. Only once there, Lacey spotted the time. She was late for her lunch date with her family at the Lodge!

"Oh no!" she cried, knowing just how seriously her mom took time keeping. "I have to go!"

The others looked at her with surprise.

"Now?" Gina asked.

"Lunch. With my family, remember?"

This was about the worst interruption Lacey could've wanted. Not only was she dreading the lunch because she knew her mom and sister had a lot to get off their chests about Frank, but she'd also missed her one opportunity to buy a second pregnancy test. Add to that the very real possibility a thief had been in her store, and it was a melting pot of stress for Lacey.

"I'm going to have to trust you guys to check the footage," Lacey said, swiping up her keys. "And to mind the store and Brother

Benedict. Do you think between the three of you, you can do that? Or do I need to leave Chester in case?"

"We can do it," Gina said, testily.

Though the events of the morning had left Lacey doubtful, she really had no other choice. Surely between the pensioner, the PhD student, the silent monk, and the arthritic dog they could keep her store safe?

"Okay," she relented. She hurried for the door, Chester coming along after her. When she reached it, she paused and looked back. "I almost forgot. I'm expecting a call from Professor Crispin Noble. If he calls, transfer him to me, please."

In all the drama, she'd forgotten just how excited she was to find out what Crispin Noble had discovered about the scepter.

"We'll transfer him straight to your cell," Finnbar replied with a nod.

"Thank you," Lacey said. "And when you find something on the cameras, text it to me."

"*If*," Gina interjected.

"*When*," Lacey replied. She was utterly convinced someone had tried to steal the scepter, and she was confident who the surveillance footage would show doing it. The treasure hunter.

But for now she had to put all of that out of her mind, because there was a huge hurdle to overcome first…

Lunch with her family!

CHAPTER TWELVE

Lacey pulled into the parking lot at the Lodge, her mind ticking over her myriad woes: Family arguments. Pregnancy worries. A possible thief. There was so much on her plate at the moment, she could feel herself becoming increasingly stressed and wound up. She really didn't want to be on edge at her wedding.

She killed her car's engine and headed inside the inn with Chester, waving a hurried hello to Lucia, who was manning the reception desk. When she reached the dining room door, she took a moment, a deep breath to steady herself, then went inside.

The dining room at the Lodge was very large, a beautiful old room with polished wooden floors that Lacey had unearthed during her interior design contract. The vast space was decorated with lots of vintage wooden tables and candelabras, and natural light poured in through the glass doors at the end. The view through it stretched out across the lawns, to the cliffs and to the ocean beyond. Even on a gray, drizzly winter's day there was no denying it was a gorgeous view.

Though the room appeared to be fully booked with diners, and bustling with noise and activity, the Lodge's dining room was a lovely, tranquil place for lunch. Lacey thought it was a shame she was too on edge to actually enjoy it.

She spotted her family over by the windows and was about to head in that direction when her attention was caught by a single diner sitting at one of the tables smaller tables near the swing-door entrance the servers used to go in and out of the kitchen. It was none other than the fake Crispin Noble, the so-called treasure hunter!

Lacey's temper immediately flared. Though she hadn't yet received confirmation from Finnbar and Gina that the man was her culprit, instinct told her he was.

She instantly changed direction and marched toward him, ready to give him a piece of her mind.

As she got closer, she saw that the treasure hunter was leaning to the side and conversing with another diner on the next table over.

“I found Jacobite gold at Loch Arkaig,” he was saying, bragging to the other diner, a smug look on his face. “Treasure lost since 1745! It’s going to earn me a fortune!”

Lacey drew up to the table and folded her arms. She glared down at him. “You!” she cried. “You thief!”

The diner on the table over cast a wary glance at Lacey, before leaning back from the treasure hunter and averting his eyes.

The treasure hunter looked up at her and smiled. “We meet again. I don’t think I had a chance to introduce myself properly. My name is Greg Ford and—”

“I don’t care who you are,” Lacey snapped, cutting him off. “I want to know what you’re still doing in Wilfordshire. I already told you the scepter’s not for sale. Are you hanging around so you can steal it?”

“It’s a free country,” Greg replied simply. He gave her a smug look. “And I’ve no need to try and steal the scepter, since I have something you need. Knowledge. I’m hanging around because I know at some point you’ll change your mind and come crawling to me for help.”

The arrogance! Lacey thought as her hands involuntarily clenched into fists. “I don’t need you. I have actual scholars working on the scepter. So why don’t you buzz off back to wherever you came from and leave me alone?”

Greg Ford looked completely unaffected by her outburst. “No, I think I’ll stay here, at this fine inn. I’ve nowhere to be in a hurry, and it’s best I’m nearby when you change your mind and realize my terms are worth it. Wisdom for a small percentage of the fee is a very reasonable exchange.”

“It’s not for sale!” Lacey cried. “I told you that already!”

She was getting increasingly riled, and now people all over the dining room were starting to look. Great, another public spat. Just what she needed.

Suddenly, Naomi was there beside her. “What’s going on?” she asked, looking confused.

Greg the treasure hunter just smirked. “I was trying to have a quiet lunch when I was accosted by this woman.”

Naomi tugged on Lacey’s arm. “Come on, let’s go.”

“Stay away from the scepter,” Lacey warned the treasure hunter one last time. “And stay away from my store.”

As Naomi dragged her away, the man just smirked.

They reached the table and Lacey sat heavily down in her dining chair. She couldn't help but keep glancing angrily at the treasure hunter on the other side of the room.

Meanwhile, Shirley, Frankie, and Naomi seemed unable to stop staring *at her*. Same for what seemed like every single diner in the restaurant. Lacey's altercation with the treasure hunter had been seen by many, and she slunk down in her seat with embarrassment.

"What was that all about?" Shirley asked, looking perplexed.

Lacey huffed. She was still fuming. "That awful man is trying to trick me. He pretended to be a scholar to get close to an antique I'm valuing at the moment. And now he's hanging around town. I don't trust him. I think he's trying to steal it from me."

She checked her phone to see if Finnbar and Gina had found any surveillance footage. Still no message. Then she spotted the signal bar was empty. Typical the Lodge would be a cell phone black spot just when she needed it!

"Ugh, hold on a minute," she said, standing. "I just need to check something."

But before she could leave, Naomi thunked a hand down on top of hers, pinning her to the table and stopping her in her tracks.

"Will you sit down!" she commanded. "You've come in here all guns a-blazing like a madwoman."

"Oh, have I?" Lacey shot back, thudding down into her seat.

"What is going on with you?" Naomi asked.

She looked astonished. In fact, they all did. Lacey was usually the calm one of the bunch; it was very rare for her to have public outbursts like this. And it wasn't just the treasure hunter who was contributing to her stress, it was everything. Her pregnancy fears. Her parents' altercation. It was all just too much.

"Have some wine," Shirley said. "You look like you need it."

Lacey thought of the possibility she might be pregnant. She shook her head. "No.

"How about some bread, Aunty Lacey?" Frankie said, offering her the basket of rolls.

It was a very sweet gesture.

"Thank you," Lacey said, picking one up and taking a big, furious bite. She recognized the taste right away as Tom's bread roll recipe—light and delicate with a hint of sugar. The taste comforted her. Her anger started to fade.

"Okay, I think I've calmed down now," she said.

"Good," Shirley said. "That was all a bit embarrassing."

As fast as it had gone, Lacey's anger came back in a sudden rush. "I'm embarrassing?" she exclaimed. "Me? You were the one standing in the middle of my high street screaming at your ex-husband!"

"Well, what do you expect?" Shirley retorted. "I haven't breathed the same air as him for over thirty years. And honestly, Lacey, I don't think I ever want to again. I'll be civil for your wedding but that's it. I never want to be in the same room as him again. I think we should cancel the dinner tonight."

Lacey gritted her teeth. "The dinner is happening."

"Why?" Shirley demanded. "So your father can ignore my questions again?"

"Well, that depends on how you ask them," Lacey replied. "Are you planning on screaming them into his face, or do you think you can use an appropriate indoor voice?"

"Indoor voice!" Frankie said with a giggle. "That's what my old kindergarten teacher used to call it."

Shirley narrowed her eyes at Lacey. "I don't appreciate that tone, young lady, nor you implying I'm acting like a child. That man called me silly."

"'*That man,*'" Lacey said, air-quoting her mother, "is my father. Whether you like it or not, you and he procreated, and made this happen!" She pointed at herself and Naomi, who was now burying her face in her hands again. "Which means traditionally speaking, he gets to walk me down the aisle on my wedding day. That's just the way it works. Your dad walked you down the aisle, and now my dad is walking me down the aisle, and you don't get to take that away from me."

Shirley huffed. "He can walk you anywhere you want, that's no concern of mine. I just don't want to have dinner with the man."

"The man," Frankie echoed, with a giggle. "He sounds like the bad guy from a comic book."

"He is," Shirley said. "That's exactly what he is."

"Mom!" Naomi hissed, peeping out through her fingers. "Don't turn Frankie against his grandad."

"Me?" Shirley exclaimed. "You're the one who pretended he didn't even have one!"

Lacey felt her anger rising and rising through her. If this bickering went on much longer she'd blow.

“Stop,” she said. “Please. Just stop. I really want to have a nice wedding. Is that too much to ask? And in order to have a nice wedding, I really need you guys to all meet up with each other first and let out a bit of this steam. The dinner is going ahead.”

She stood, discarded the piece of bread she’d barely picked at on the table. Her frayed nerves could take no more. Enough was enough.

“Where are you going?” Shirley asked, looking at her eldest daughter with a stunned expression.

“I’m leaving,” Lacey replied. “Before I say something I regret. I hope you enjoy your lunch.”

She quickly marched away before Shirley got a chance to say anything else. Lacey knew her limits, and knew when she was close to blowing. If she shouted at her mom, Shirley would hold a grudge for at least a week, and being given the silent treatment by her mother on her wedding day would be a disaster.

Lacey made it out into the parking lot of the Lodge, the cold night air cooling her hot, angry cheeks. As soon as she made it down the steps and to the gravel lot, her phone pinged. She had signal again, and a message had come in.

She checked her screen. The message was from Finnbar.

You were right! Someone tried to get into the safe. But we couldn’t see their face. They were wearing a mask.

A mask, eh? Lacey thought, glancing back at the Lodge, where Greg Ford was still sitting inside smugly enjoying his lunch. *Sneaky.*

She quickly texted back, feeling vindicated that there was now irrefutable evidence to back up what she knew to be true. *Good work. On my way. I’ll call the cops.*

Greg might have tried to hide his identity, but it would take more than a mask to fool Lacey.

CHAPTER THIRTEEN

Lacey arrived back at her store at the same time the cop cruiser pulled up.

"Someone called about an attempted robbery?" the male officer said as he emerged out of the front seat onto the sidewalk.

"That was me," Lacey replied. "This way."

She led the male officer and his female partner inside the store. Finnbar and Gina were at the counter, eyes glued to the TV screen as they watched the surveillance footage on playback.

"Oh, Lacey," Finnbar said when he spotted her. "Here. Come and look."

Lacey went behind the counter, the officers following. They were like sardines packed in behind there, and they all craned their heads to look up at the screen.

Finnbar hit play, and the screen filled with the image of the shop floor. There was Lacey, hurrying to the door with Chester in tow. She exited, and barely a minute later, Gina left the shop floor herself, heading to the back room.

Lacey couldn't help but narrow her eyes and glare at the woman. Sixty seconds was all it had taken for her to go against Lacey's command to mind the store while she ran a quick errand. Couldn't she have just waited for Finnbar to arrive?

But there was no chance to give her a piece of her mind, because almost as soon as Gina was out of sight, a figure crept in through the door. He'd clearly been lying in wait, watching, spying, and waiting for his moment. He was wearing a mask, and his features were entirely obscured.

Lacey shuddered. The footage was very chilling.

She watched as Boudica raised her head. The figure threw something to her. A dog treat? That's all it had taken to get Boo not to raise the alarm?

"He's familiar with the store," Lacey commented. "If he knows we have guard dogs."

That was one check mark in the Greg Ford box. The other was the fact the figure was clearly male—his height and movements gave him away. The other tell-tale clue was the fact he beelined straight for the back room where the safe was.

Finnbar clicked a button to change the view, tracking the treasure hunter as he went into the storeroom and over to the safe. He produced a crow bar, laying it on top of the safe as he crouched down and started fiddling with the lock.

"That bastard!" Lacey cried, bringing her hands into fists. "I knew it!"

The male cop looked at her. "You recognize this person?" he asked, sounding skeptical that someone in a mask could be identified.

"Yes," Lacey said. "It's Greg Ford."

Gina and Finnbar exchanged a glance.

"Who's Greg Ford?" Finnbar asked.

"The treasure hunter," Lacey replied. "I'm sure it's him. He came in here this morning impersonating a scholar, and he saw where my safe was. He probably only came to get the lay of the land in the first place. I was the one who asked him if he was Crispin Noble, and he must've just gone along with it to get a closer look at the scepter. Maybe even to spy over my shoulder to get the combination for the lock."

She felt furious and foolish that the man had hoodwinked her so thoroughly.

She looked at the cops. "He has a room at the Lodge. You should arrest him."

The male cop frowned. His female partner raised an eyebrow.

"We don't arrest people without evidence," she said, condescendingly.

Lacey gestured to the surveillance screen, where Greg Ford had abandoned his attempts to crack the combination and was now attempting to prize open the door with his crowbar. "What's that, if not evidence?"

"Well," the male cop began, "what we have here is a figure walking into an open and unmanned store. So no break-in. He then leaves with nothing. So no robbery. The most criminal thing that's happened here is an attempt to damage property."

Lacey narrowed her eyes. "Are you actually kidding right now? I know exactly who that is and exactly what he's doing and you're going to let him go scot-free?"

The cop shook his head. "No. We'll investigate. But we can't just take your word at it and arrest a man because you think you recognize him. That could be anyone. Could even be a woman. A chancer who came off the street when they noticed the store was empty."

Lacey was furious. "A chancer doesn't walk in off the street with a crowbar and mask, head straight for the safe, and leave behind everything else of value!"

The cops weren't listening. They headed back around the counter and headed for the door.

"Ma'am, let us do our jobs our way," the man said.

"Well, how long will you take?" Lacey said, hands on hips.

"This is extremely low priority," the female replied. "We have real criminals to be dealing with."

"We'll be in touch," the man added.

And with that, they left.

Lacey stood there fuming. "What a waste of time they are!" she cried.

She marched for the back room.

"What are you doing?" Gina asked, as she and Finnbar hurried after her.

Lacey stopped at the safe and unlocked it, then removed the crate containing the scepter. "If I can't trust the cops to do their jobs, then I'm not leaving this behind. It's too risky."

She straightened up.

"Are you going somewhere?" Gina asked.

"Yes," Lacey said, holding her head high. "If the cops won't do anything, then I'm taking matters into my own hands." She whistled for Chester. "Come on, boy. It's time to pay a visit to a treasure hunter."

*

Lacey marched up to the front desk of the Lodge. Lucia was on duty, and she eyed her warily.

"Is everything okay?" she asked.

Lacey was riled, and it was clearly showing on her face.

"Your family went back to their rooms a few minutes ago," Lucia continued. "Do you want me to call them down?"

Lacey shook her head. "I'm here to see Greg Ford," she said. "Is he still in the dining room?"

Lucia looked even more bemused. "Um, no. No one is. The lunch shift is over. There's no one in the dining room anymore. Lacey, is everything okay?"

“Do you know where he went?” Lacey asked. “Did he check out?”

Lucia shrugged. “I didn’t see him leave, so I assume he’s on the grounds somewhere.”

Lacey paused, mulling it over.

Perhaps her outburst earlier had scared him? Even though he’d seemed totally unfazed by it, perhaps she’d actually managed to rattle him. She’d accused him of being a thief to his face, after all, and that accusation had now been corroborated with evidence. And even if the cops weren’t going to act particularly quickly, *he* didn’t know that. Perhaps he’d realized that now she was on to him, it wouldn’t be long before she gathered the necessary evidence against him. If she’d been in his position, she would’ve fled as soon as she could too.

Only, Lucia hadn’t seen him leave. He hadn’t checked out. That meant he was still here, somewhere on the grounds. Had he taken to hiding out in the Lodge?

Lacey glanced over to the dining room, and to the big double glass doors at the end that led to the lawn. If Lucia hadn’t seen him, could it be because he went out that way? If he’d gone to his room, he would have passed her. If he’d snuck into the kitchen, the only way out from there was to go through the delivery area and the staff parking area, both of which were off limits to guests. He would be very quickly stopped if he went that way. So the only chance he’d have had to escape unnoticed was to go out the dining room doors and through the lawns…

She hurried in that direction, Chester trotting along with her.

“Lacey?” Lucia called as she went. “What’s going on?”

Lacey didn’t stop. There was no time for talk. If Greg was on the lam, then time was of the essence.

She rushed into the dining room. The tables were covered in detritus from the shift, and the many servers were busily working to tidy up. Lacey cast a quick glance at the table where her uncomfortable family meeting had taken place. The bread roll she’d discarded was still there. She grimaced at the unpleasant memory, then quickly put it all out of her mind and hurried through the patio doors and out into the lawns.

Immediately, a blast of cold wind gushed at her. Lacey shivered, and Chester began to growl. Lacey looked down at him, suddenly getting the feeling that something was off. It wasn’t like Chester to growl at the weather.

“What is it, boy?” she asked him.

He barked, his face turned from her and out toward the downward sloping lawn. Lacey got a strange, creeping sensation of goosebumps on her arms, and knew it wasn't just from the chill in the air. Chester had sensed something, and now she, too, could feel it. Something was wrong.

She began to head down the incline, taking slow, careful steps. Each step made the sense of disquiet grow stronger, and now the hairs on Chester's back were standing on end. He let out a long, low grumble, and bared his teeth.

"The bandstand," Lacey said, following the direction of his focus to the hexagonal wooden structure at the midpoint of the lawns. It was raised several feet off the ground and set in thick concrete at the base. Thanks to the position of the sun at this time of day, its shadow stretched over a large portion of the rest of the garden. Lacey got the sudden, horrible instinctive feeling that something was in that darkness. Or someone. Greg Ford, perhaps, was hiding behind the bandstand, watching her. Was that what Chester had sensed?

Holding her breath, Lacey crept ever closer to the bandstand. Chester creeped along beside her. They inched around the edges, moving silently and slowly into the dark shadow.

That's when Lacey saw it. Something lying in the grass. Not something… someone!

Lacey gasped as her eyes roved from a pair of leather shoes up to beige pants, and a checkered shirt, before landing on the dark brown hair. The person was lying face down in the grass and they weren't moving.

Heart thudding, Lacey raced to the body and grabbed it by the shoulders. It was a dead weight.

She spun them over to face her, and screamed. Looking up at her, dead and unseeing, was Greg Ford.

CHAPTER FOURTEEN

The sound of Chester's barks echoed around the lawns of the Lodge. Lacey scrambled back in the dirt, recoiling from the dead man, and managed to heave herself to her shaking legs. With trembling hands she fumbled in her pocket for her cell phone and tugged it out. She could barely see what she was doing as she punched in the number of the local police station.

The call connected. "Yes ma'am?" a weary voice said.

Lacey drew in a ragged breath, about to request DCI Lewis and Superintendent Turner's assistance, but faltered. *Ma'am? How had they known she was a ma'am before she'd even spoken?*

"I'm calling about a—" she began.

"—robbery?" the operator interrupted. "Yes, yes. We have the report and there are officers assigned, it's just a very busy day today."

Lacey frowned. Did they have her cell phone number stored in caller ID? "This is nothing to do with a robbery."

"No?" the woman asked, sounding very uninterested. "What's happened now? Someone's graffitied your shed? Stolen your potted plants out of the greenhouse?"

Lacey's mouth dropped open with astonishment. This was absolutely deplorable! Clearly, the local station had decided she was a time waster and flagged her cell phone number. Of course, she did phone them very regularly, but not because she was some local busybody hassling them over insignificant problems! She only ever called them for perfectly legitimate reasons, ones where she'd always been proven right in the end.

Chester's barking became more and more shrill.

"I need Beth Lewis and Karl Turner at the Lodge ASAP," Lacey said, pressing a finger in her other ear to block out the noise.

"Why?" the operator asked, sounding surprised, presumably because she was firstly asking for the murder detectives, and secondly that she knew them on a first-name basis.

"There's been a murder!" Lacey exclaimed.

By now, Chester's frantic barks had alerted the guests and staff of the Lodge to the unfolding situation. People started appearing at the windows, peeping through curtains, craning their heads to see what was happening. The servers who'd been tidying the dining room minutes earlier began to gather on the back steps, huddling and talking urgently to each other. Then Lacey spotted Lucia and Suzy come flying through the patio doors and push their way through the cluster of servers. They started racing down the sloped lawn toward her.

"What makes you so certain there's been a murder?" she heard the operator in her ear. Her nasally voice and suspicious mannerisms made Lacey bristle.

"The dead body lying at my feet," Lacey replied. "It's a bit of a giveaway."

Her sassy comment wasn't going to do her any favors, but Lacey couldn't help it. She was sick of being treated so dismissively by law enforcement. First the cops at her store, now the operator at the station. Not to mention Superintendent Turner, who'd always seemed to have it out for her.

Suzy and Lucia reached her. They saw the dead body and gasped.

Suzy immediately sprang into action, grabbing her phone and dialing the cops. "There's been a murder!" she cried, before looking at Lucia. "Lock the hotel down. Make sure none of the guests can see this."

A shocked-looking Lucia nodded and scurried back away.

Still clutching the phone to her ear, Suzy looked at Lacey next. "The cops are on their way."

Lacey couldn't help but be a little annoyed that Suzy's operator had leapt into action while hers had treated her like the boy who cried wolf.

She spoke into her own cell phone. "Don't worry. There are already cops on the way," she told the mean operator. She promptly hung up before she heard another sarcastic reply.

Suzy crouched down next to Greg Ford's lifeless body. "Did you see what happened?"

Lacey shook her head. "No."

The sound of sirens came from the distance.

Suzy peered up at Lacey. "What are you still doing here? I thought you were coming for lunch."

"I did. Then I left. Then I came back just now."

Suzy narrowed her eyes. Lacey couldn't blame her. Her movements that day certainly seemed convoluted. Back and forth and back again.

"Why did you come back?" Suzy asked.

Lacey pointed at the dead man. "To see him, actually."

Suzy looked aghast. “You know him? He’s a friend of yours?”

“Friend?” Lacey scoffed. “Absolutely not. He tried to break into my safe, and I came here to confront him with the evidence.”

Suzy looked perplexed. It was a lot to take in. Lacey was trying to get her head around it all as well.

But there was no time to explain further because the sound of sirens came screaming right up to the Lodge, blue lights illuminating everything. A moment later, the cops came trooping through the open dining room doors, a terrified-looking Lucia pointing them in the right direction. They raced down the sloped lawns toward Lacey, Suzy, Chester, and the dead body of Greg Ford. DCI Lewis and Superintendent Turner, the murder detectives, brought up the rear. Superintendent Turner was in his usual beige trench coat, his shock of white hair poking out over his turned up collar. Beth’s honey blond hair was styled in her usual ballerina bun, and she was dressed down in black loafers, slacks, and a long khaki jacket.

Superintendent Turner went straight to the body, crouched down, and began examining it from all angles. He clicked his fingers at the uniformed officers beside him. “Secure the scene.”

As the dreaded blue crime scene tape went up around the bandstand and beyond, DCI Lewis came over to Lacey and Suzy.

“What’s going on?” she asked, removing her notebook and pen from her breast pocket. She clicked the lid.

“He’s a guest,” Suzy explained, gesturing to the dead man. “Greg Ford.”

“So not a local?” Beth confirmed. “Any idea why he’s staying in Wilfordshire?”

“He’s a treasure hunter,” Lacey offered. “He came because I have an antique he wants. He pretended to be an archaeological scholar to get close to it, but when that failed, he attempted to steal it from my safe. I confronted him about it but didn’t have the evidence to back it up. By the time I got the evidence and came back here… he was dead.”

As she’d been speaking, Beth’s eyes had started to narrow as if in doubt. Now her expression was full-on disbelief.

“Go through that one more time,” she said. “Slower.”

This time, Superintendent Turner decided to join them, clearly interested in what Lacey had to say on the matter. He stood with his hands in the pockets of his long trench coat, towering over Lacey with his huge six-foot-three frame.

Lacey felt her nerves spike. She took a deep breath and recounted the events once more. On her second iteration she realized just how bad she sounded. Accusing a man of theft? Tarnishing his reputation? Confronting him?

…And then being the first to discover his lifeless body…

She gulped. This didn't look good for her. It didn't look good at all.

A horrible sense of déjà vu came over her. She had been through this now so many times, and couldn't help but wonder when it would all end. The feeling of anxiety and doom was too familiar now, washing over her like an old, unwanted emotion.

"Lacey," Superintendent Turner said stiffly when she was done. "Are you saying this is related to the attempted theft you reported this morning?"

"Yes," she said. "This is the perpetrator."

"And he's the same man you were seen arguing with in the dining room at lunch today?" Superintendent Turner pressed.

Lacey squirmed. How did he know about that? The only way he knew about that was if the cops investigating the burglary had discovered it while questioning witnesses and passed it on. The fight would make her look even worse!

"That's right," she said.

"The same man you demanded my team arrest. Even though you had no evidence."

She bit her lip. "Uh-huh."

Superintendent Turner let out a long, slow exhalation and swiped a hand through his slicked back gray hair.

"Look, I know what you're thinking," Lacey blurted. "But I have nothing to do with this! I didn't do anything!"

"I know that," Superintendent Turner snapped. "You have a pretty good track record of not being a murderer."

Lacey paused. She frowned with confusion. Superintendent Turner *wasn't* accusing her? That wasn't like him at all! He usually leapt to an immediate conclusion.

"You… you know it wasn't me?" she echoed, uncertain and not wanting to jinx it.

"Yes," he barked again.

"Then what's the problem?" Lacey asked.

"The problem," he replied, testily, "is that you're always getting in the way of my investigations!"

"By solving them," Lacey said.

"Yes. But that's beside the point. You've made a hell of a lot of paperwork for me throughout my career. I can't say I'm going to miss it."

Lacey paused. It sunk in what he was saying. "You're retiring?"

He nodded stiffly. He appeared to be on the verge of getting emotional but managed to reel it back in and set his face firmly.

"Last case," he said, rocking on his heels. "Fitting it would be another one of yours and Fido's." He nodded to Chester. Then he looked back at Lacey. "Look. Can you just do me this one favor? Keep your nose out of this case. Let me solve it on my own, my own way, without you interfering and getting me in hot water with the higher-ups."

The sleuth in Lacey wanted to rebuff. But she also had to accept looking into the case was more than she could handle right now. Wedding. Family. Possible pregnancy. The scepter. She had more than enough to handle without adding a murder investigation into the mix.

"Okay," she said. "You can consider it my retirement gift."

Superintendent Turner smiled—*actually smiled*—for the first time Lacey could recall.

"Thank you," he said. "Now, you know the drill. You're our star witness, which means you can't leave town until this investigation is over."

Lacey was about to say "no problem," but stopped. Because it suddenly dawned on her that her wedding was outside of Wilfordshire, taking place in the forest. Her stomach plummeted. She shook her head. "I have to be able to leave town. My wedding is in two days! It's outside of Wilfordshire!"

Superintendent Turner took another deep, weary sigh. He shook his head. "I'm sorry, Lacey. I can't help you with that. You're the prime witness. We'll need to question you in the coming days. Several times. It sounds like our victim has a complicated history of deceit and petty crime. I suspect he's made many enemies through his lifetime. Your information will be vital."

"But…" Lacey stammered. "But that means if it's not solved in the next forty-eight hours, I won't be able to go to my own wedding!" She looked at Beth. The female detective was invited. Maybe she'd be able to talk some sense into the superintendent. "Beth? Tell him."

But Beth looked awkward. Her gaze dropped to the floor. "Sorry, Lacey. Rules are rules."

Lacey's stomach fell to her toes. Was she going to have to cancel her wedding?

CHAPTER FIFTEEN

"Lacey!" a voice called across the lawn.

Lacey swirled on the spot to see her mom and Naomi charging toward her. It was dark now, and Lacey had been standing in the grounds of the Lodge for hours while the police worked.

Poor Lucia was still attempting to guard the patio doors, and she looked flustered that Shirley and Naomi had simply barged right past her.

"Stop!" the cops at the perimeter of the blue cordon shouted. "This is a crime scene!"

Lacey hurried up to them. "They're my family."

"What's going on?" Shirley cried.

"There's a dead man," Lacey said. "Murdered."

Naomi gasped. "And you found him?"

Lacey nodded.

"Oh no," Shirley said, before adding, leadingly, "I guess that means we'll have to cancel dinner."

"What?" Lacey said. Was that really her mom's first concern? Was she really going to use this as an excuse to cancel their reunion dinner?

"I'm just saying, we can't exactly have dinner now!" Shirley replied. "I don't know about you two, but knowing a man was killed a few feet away from my hotel window makes me feel somewhat queasy."

It was a good point. Lacey felt too sick to eat—it would probably take a long time to get her appetite back after seeing Greg's dead body—and the wedding might not even be able to go ahead. If all anyone was actually going to do was yell at each other, then Lacey might be better off avoiding the dinner altogether.

"You're right," Lacey said, relenting. "I'll call Dad to cancel. Just as soon as I'm allowed to leave."

Naomi looked down at the police tape separating them with consternation. "Why are they keeping you in there?"

"I was the first to find the body," she said. "And I touched it. They have to make sure the scene matches up with my statement before I can go."

“Are you a suspect?” Naomi asked, eyes widening, whispering the last word.

Lacey shook her head. “For once, no,” she said.

Shirley looked perturbed. “What do you mean for once?”

“Long story,” Lacey said, her gaze darting over to Superintendent Turner, who was busy placing a crime scene marker next to a piece of evidence in the grass. She turned back to her worried-looking mom and sister. “Don’t worry,” she said. “I’ll be okay.”

Naomi tightened her arms around her stomach. “How can you be so sure? There’s a murderer on the loose.”

Lacey squeezed her arm. “There are two really good detectives on the case.”

Naomi nodded and glanced behind her at the Lodge, her gaze going up to the top windows where many patrons were gazing out in shock. “Luckily Frankie’s asleep right now. But what happens when he wakes up and sees all the police activity? The crime scene tape? The forensic tent? Then what? I don’t want him finding out about this.”

Lacey felt terrible for her. “Come back with me tonight,” she said, looking from her sister to her mom. “All of you.”

Naomi looked surprised. “Are you sure? It’s two nights before your wedding.”

“I thought you said you didn’t want us ‘crowding your style,’” Shirley added, using air quotes.

“That really does not sound like the sort of thing I’d say, does it?” Lacey contested. “And I only didn’t want you guys around because it was going to be crazy busy at the cottage, and I wanted you all to get comfortable nights’ sleep here. But the circumstances have changed. I won’t want you staying in an inn where you don’t feel safe. So come home with me. It’s obviously for the best.”

She hadn’t been able to go back for the second pregnancy test, so it wasn’t like she needed the privacy of the evening to herself anymore. And even if she had bought one, this was more important. Her family’s well-being came first.

Naomi bit her lip. She obviously didn’t want to be an imposition so close to the wedding, but little did she know, the wedding was looking unlikely to go ahead anyway.

“Are you sure you’re sure?” she asked.

“I’m sure,” Lacey said, smiling.

Naomi gave her a grateful smile. “Okay, thanks. I’ll go pack our cases.”

Lacey glanced at the cop guarding the cordon. "I don't know how long I'll stay here, but I'll meet you in the parking lot as soon as I'm allowed to go." She looked at her mother. "Mom? Are you coming too?"

Shirley was busy fiddling with her cell phone. She looked up, snapping to attention. "Yes. Yes, I'm coming," she said.

Naomi took her mother's arm, and they headed back up the lawn toward the Lodge. As she watched them go, Lacey's phone started to ring.

She took it from her pocket and saw Tom's name flashing up at her. She paced away and answered.

"Lacey?" came Tom's urgent voice in her ear. "What's going on? Is everything okay? Your mom just texted me to say someone was murdered at the Lodge!"

Lacey glowered at the back of her mom as she disappeared in through the patio doors. So that's what she'd been going on her phone—texting Tom! Typical of her to go and tell him before Lacey herself had the chance to.

"I'm okay," she assured him. "Everything's fine."

"Do you need me to come pick you up?" he asked. He sounded stressed, which was exactly the last thing Lacey wanted her soon-to-be-groom to be feeling right now, and the main reason she hadn't immediately contacted him.

"No," Lacey said quickly. Now that the pharmacist had explained that the inconclusive test was most likely positive, there was no way she could keep it from Tom. But with everything going on right now, she just wasn't ready to speak to him about it.

"Are you sure?" he asked, sounding confused.

"I promise. Mom, Naomi, and Frankie are going to come and stay with me tonight. So I won't be on my own. And it will be pretty hectic."

On the other end of the line, there was a long pause. When Tom spoke again, there was an edge of anguish in his voice. "Lacey, are you avoiding me?"

A guilty pit opened inside of Lacey as realized she had indeed been avoiding him. Because of the pregnancy scare and not knowing how or what to tell him. And now she had even worse news to break to him—that the wedding might be called off!

"I've just been super busy," she said. "With…stuff."

"What stuff? The monk?"

"Yes, among other things."

"And you're sure it's not because I saw you in your wedding dress? Because I looked into it and it's only bad luck the *night before.* I think Gina's worried you over nothing."

"Good to know," Lacey said.

Just then, one of the cops approached her. She covered the mouthpiece with her hand.

"You're allowed to leave," he said. "Turner wants me to remind you not to leave town and keep your phone on in case he needs to contact you over anything."

Lacey nodded. "Thank you." She removed her hand. "Tom, I have to go. But I'll come to the patisserie tomorrow so we can…talk."

He sighed. "Okay. Speak soon."

And with that, the call cut out.

Lacey felt her shoulders slump with disappointment. That wasn't how she liked to end calls with Tom. She felt awful for avoiding him.

As she ducked beneath the police tape and headed for the parking lot, she decided that tomorrow morning she would be brave and tell Tom everything.

But first things first, she had to collect her family and settle them in at the cottage.

CHAPTER SIXTEEN

"Have you all got everything?" Lacey asked from the stable door in the kitchen of Crag Cottage.

From the round window table her weary-looking mother and sister nodded. They were in their pajamas. Lacey's were tucked under her arm. It had taken her approximately five minutes after walking in through her front door before realizing there was no way they'd all comfortably fit inside and she'd be better off having a sleepover at Gina's.

"Will you come around in the morning to make breakfast?" Shirley asked.

Lacey tensed. She'd planned on waking early to see Tom and discuss all the shenanigans going on before they opened their respective stores for the day. She didn't have time to fit in making breakfast for three people!

"I can't," she said. "I have an early morning. You want me to wake you up at five?"

Shirley grimaced.

"Didn't think so," Lacey replied. "You should all sleep in." She was saying it as much for herself as for them. "And then walk Chester down the beach to the store once you're all rested."

She'd decided that leaving Chester with them was the best course of action. He would be a security guard, and hopefully make them feel more at ease while there was a murderer out there.

"Fine," Shirley replied. "Goodnight."

"Goodnight." Lacey leaned down and ruffled Chester's head. "You take care of everyone, okay, boy?"

He yapped.

Lacey headed out into the dark night and trudged across the lawn to the gap in the hedge between Gina's and her properties. She squeezed through, then maneuvered through the sheep, and knocked on Gina's door.

The top half of the stable door swung inward and the older woman's face appeared in the gap.

"Lacey?" she asked, adjusting her bright red plastic spectacles. "What are you doing here?"

"Sleepover?" Lacey asked, showing her friend the pajamas and wash bag under her arm.

"Of course," Gina said, unlocking the bottom half of the door to allow her entrance. "But why? What's wrong with your house?"

"I have some guests…" Lacey said,

"Your family?" Gina guessed. "What happened? You were adamant they weren't going to stay."

"It's a long story," Lacey said, stepping inside.

Gina nodded. "In that case, I'll put the kettle on."

Lacey flopped down at the table, suddenly bone tired after the day she'd had. As Gina made the tea, she relayed everything that had happened at the Lodge that evening.

"No!" Gina exclaimed, her mouth wide open as she put the teapot down on the table. "He was murdered?"

Lacey nodded sadly. "The cops seem to think it has something to do with his treasure hunting. That maybe he was some kind of criminal. They want to know all about my association with him."

Gina rolled her eyes. "They suspect you? What a surprise."

"Actually, no," Lacey said. "Not this time. Turns out Superintendent Turner is retiring. This is his last case. He's decided I'm an important witness. I still can't leave town though."

"But the wedding?" Gina said. "It's in less than two days. They're not going to be able to solve it in two days!"

"It's unlikely," Lacey said, nodding sadly.

Gina seemed to grasp the situation. "Oh. Oh. You're thinking…"

"…I might have to cancel the wedding," Lacey said. "No forest. No gold harp." She twisted her engagement band on her finger mournfully. "No Mrs. Forrester."

Gina shook her head. "That absolutely won't do. I've worked too hard to have this fall apart at the last second!" She slapped her hands with determination on the table. "There will be a wedding one way or another."

Lacey looked at her skeptically. "Really? What are you going to do? Make a plan B wedding?"

"Exactly!" Gina exclaimed.

Lacey wasn't convinced. But at least it gave Gina something to focus on.

She stood. "All right, dear. You do that. I'm off to bed."

Gina wasn't listening anymore. She was in full-blown action mode!

As Lacey trudged up the wooden staircase, she thought ahead to tomorrow, and the talk she needed to have with Tom.

CHAPTER SEVENTEEN

Lacey woke in Gina's spare room the next morning feeling like an anxious ball of nervous worry.

It was supposed to be the day before her wedding, but now she didn't even know if that wedding was going to happen!

Her mind was full of worries as she readied herself for the day. Down in the kitchen, she discovered Gina asleep at the kitchen table, a stack of papers acting as a pillow. She must've dropped off in the middle of trying to reorganize the wedding.

Lacey smiled to herself, touched that her friend cared so much, then headed out into the cold early morning.

As she walked across the lawn, she glanced up at the windows of Crag Cottage. Inside, all was dark and still. Hopefully, her family would have a long, long lie-in, and give her the space she needed this morning to get her ducks in a row. She still had to source a second pregnancy test, and tell Tom all about it. And worse, she had to break the news about their nuptials.

Her chest heavy with emotion, Lacey hopped into her secondhand car and drove to town. It felt odd not having Brother Benedict in the passenger seat. She'd quickly grown accustomed to her escort, but all the guests at the Lodge were on lockdown while the police carried on their investigation.

More noticeably absent was Chester. Lacey almost felt lost without her sidekick. A little vulnerable, even. But it was more important he stay with her family and give them some assurance in this difficult time. Lacey had dealt with murderers before, but they never had, and this was clearly affecting them. Or, at least Naomi. Shirley never seemed too concerned about anyone outside of herself.

Lacey reached the pharmacy, noticing its steel shutters were still down. She squinted, spotting a sign attached to them. *"Closed till midday,"* the sign read. *"Sorry for any inconvenience."*

Lacey sighed. She felt a mixture of apprehension and relief. She wanted to get the pregnancy test out of the way, but at the same time, she didn't know how well she'd cope now if it turned out positive. There was even more stress to deal with than before. Perhaps it was better to stay in the dark. What you don't know can't hurt you, or so they say.

She parked in her usual side alley, then walked around the corner onto the main high street. But instead of going to the antiques store, she diverted to Tom's patisserie.

The bell tinkled overhead as she walked inside. Tom was at the counter, cleaning, his sleeves rolled up to the elbow and showing off his tanned arms.

"Lacey!" he said, looking at her with concern. "How are you?" He abandoned his cloth and raced from behind the counter to take her in his arms. "I've been so worried."

"I'm sorry," Lacey said as she folded into them and breathed in his comforting familiar scent. "I've had a lot on my mind."

He released her. "Like what? Tell me. You know you can tell me anything. I'm about to be your husband!"

Lacey's stomach turned. That was probably the best place to start, with the very real possibility they were going to have to cancel their wedding.

"About that…" Lacey began.

But before she could say more, she was suddenly interrupted by the bell going over the door. She looked behind her. A tall man walked in, grinning widely.

"Tom!" he exclaimed.

Lacey frowned. She'd never seen this man before in her life, but he was clearly a friend or acquaintance of Tom's.

She looked back at Tom. He was frowning too.

"I'm sorry, do I know you?" he asked.

The tall man bounded forward, his grin growing even wider, and took Tom's hand, shaking it up and down vigorously. "It's me!" he exclaimed. "Harry!"

Tom's eyes widened, his demeanor suddenly changing. "Harry? No way!" He looked astonished. A grin burst onto his face and he pulled the man into a tight embrace. "How the devil are you!"

Lacey watched them, completely baffled.

"Sorry, what's going on here?" she asked.

Tom seemed to suddenly remember she was there. He let go of the stranger and turned to her, looking eager and excited. "Lacey, this is Harry. Nora's cousin."

Ah yes, Nora. The ex-stepsister Tom had forgotten to tell Lacey about. And here was another relative that he'd failed to mention to her.

"So he's your ex-step-second-cousin?" she asked.

Harry guffawed. "Something like that!"

"We haven't seen each other for, what, thirty years?" Tom said.

"Thereabouts," Harry replied. "We were great friends though. Remember that vacation we took together?"

"Do you know what?" Tom said. "This is a crazy coincidence. But I just uploaded a bunch of photos to Facebook from that very vacation!"

"Somerset!" Harry cried. "Best weeks of my young life."

"Nothing but adventures back in those days, eh?" Tom commented. "Although I'm surprised you didn't end up with a chip on your shoulder. We could be pretty mean." He looked at Lacey. "We used to call him Baby Carrot because he was so short and puny, and had bright red hair." He pointed at Harry's now tall physique and dark hair. "I guess you grew out of that!"

Harry chuckled. "Yes, mine was a real ugly duckling to a beautiful swan story." He pointed out the window at a very flashy yellow sports car. "And that chip on my shoulder helped me become a very successful businessman."

"From Baby Carrot to Top Dog," Lacey commented.

Harry guffawed once again. He seemed very personable. Charming. Tom seemed to have completely lit up in his presence.

"And this must be the lucky lady!" Harry said, taking her hand and shaking it.

"This is my fiancée, Lacey," Tom said. "You heard we were engaged?"

"That's why I'm here. To say congratulations. Our side of the family are all up in Scotland now, but I heard it on the family grapevine that there was a wedding coming up in Wilfordshire, and I thought to myself, "Didn't *Tom* live in Wilfordshire?" Which obviously got me thinking about all the fun stuff we did as kids, and I thought I'd chance it. So I came here to say congratulations."

Tom looked astonished. "Funnily enough, we're actually getting married tomorrow."

Lacey squirmed, uncomfortable with the knowledge they might not actually be able to go ahead with it anymore.

"Why don't you stay overnight and come?" Tom asked. "I'll add you to the guest list."

"Really?" Harry said, looking thrilled. "I'd love that. If it's all right with your soon-to-be better half, of course?"

They both looked expectantly at Lacey. Lacey couldn't help but feel a little jealous that Tom's family was so together when hers always seemed to be at odds. But she didn't want to ruin the moment for him. He seemed happier than she'd seen him in months.

"Of course," she said. Knowing full well there might not be a wedding for Harry to come to anyway.

Tom looked at her. "What was it you wanted to tell me?"

"Nothing," Lacey said. "It can wait. You and Harry clearly have a lot of catching up to do."

She left them and headed across the street to her antiques store. As she went, she realized that she wanted exactly what Tom had—a functional family. And the wedding was the only way she had a chance at doing it. No way was she going to let this murder stop her from her happiness, from getting the wedding she'd been planning for months! Besides, think of all the drama and fighting that would happen when she told everyone it had been canceled. She'd never be able to deal with it. And as she entered her store, she realized that the murderer might very well want her scepter. She might not be safe until she found out who did it.

Suddenly, Lacey was determined. She might have promised Superintendent Turner she wouldn't get involved, but the stakes were too high. She was going to stick her nose in the case after all. She was going to solve the murder.

Lacey went straight to the counter and pulled out her notebook and pen. She started writing down everything she knew about Greg Ford and a timeline of his movements in Wilfordshire.

The first thing that struck her was how quickly the duplicitous man moved. He'd arrived in Wilfordshire the morning after her post on the archaeological society's forum. He'd attempted to steal the scepter at the very first opportunity, and brazenly, considering there were two people and a dog on site, even if all of them were absorbed with their own activities—meditating, gardening, sleeping. He'd had a crowbar and a mask, as if he'd always been planning on striking. And he'd booked a room at the Lodge in order to stay close and keep an ear to the ground. It all struck Lacey as the planning of an organized criminal.

Then there was the day of his death. He'd been equally quick that day, zipping around with Lacey barely five minutes on his tail by the looks of things. He'd managed to commit an attempted burglary at the store and then get to the Lodge in time for lunch. It wasn't an impossible feat—Lacey herself had made the journey, about five minutes behind him—but it certainly showed some forethought.

"So he made it back to the Lodge for lunch," she said. "Possibly in an attempt to establish an alibi for the attempted theft?"

And then what? He'd been killed in the short space of time it had taken her to return to her store, talk to the cops, and come back to the Lodge to challenge him again. Whoever had wanted him dead must've been pretty determined. They might well have acted almost immediately after his attempt to escape out the back dining room exit. In fact, they seemed just as fast as Greg himself was.

Lacey pondered it all, trying to fit all the pieces together in her mind.

Suddenly, she remembered how she'd overhead Greg talking—no, bragging—to the man on the table over. Something to do with long-lost Jacobite gold?

What if the guest he'd been bragging to was the killer? Perhaps he'd killed him to get his gold?

She decided her first step was to go to the Lodge to question the staff there about the man dining on the table next to Greg. She'd leave just as soon as Gina arrived.

Speak of the devil, in came Gina. She had Boudica weaving around at her feet, and Naomi, Shirley, Frankie, and Chester in tow.

Great, Lacey thought. She'd really hoped she'd have a bit more time before her family descended.

Shirley looked utterly thrilled this morning. She was clearly still on a high from the cancelled dinner. Naomi, on the other hand, looked weary. Her mind was clearly more on the dead man found at the inn they were staying at. Frankie seemed oblivious to all the drama, and Lacey was glad they'd managed to keep him out of it all so far.

Chester ran over to greet her as they all bustled inside chatting loudly.

"Morning, Aunty Lacey!" Frankie shouted, ruffling Chester's fur.

"We thought you might prefer to have breakfast here," Shirley said.

"Actually, I just have to step out," Lacey said.

Shirley's face dropped. "Now, Lacey. You left before lunch. Then dinner was cancelled. We absolutely must have breakfast. When else will we get the time to catch up before the wedding?"

Lacey felt bad for blowing them off. But if she didn't act now, there would be no wedding to go to!

Frankie gazed up at her from where he was ruffling Chester's fur. "Gina said she'd cover," he added, hopefully.

His big puppy dog eyes made Lacey feel even worse.

"I'm sorry," she said. "I just have some really important last-minute preparations to go through at the Lodge. I can't put it off."

Frankie pouted, looking downcast.

"But I'm sure Gina can entertain you until I'm back?" Lacey added. "Maybe you could do some gardening together?"

"Great idea, boss," Gina said, giving her a knowing look. She probably assumed Lacey was rushing off to make arrangements for the secret wedding Plan B, and Lacey wasn't about to tell her what she was really up to. "Want to help me in the greenhouse, Frankie?"

He brightened and gave her a nod.

"Thank you," Lacey mouthed to Gina.

Her friend nodded, took hold of the little boy's hand, and headed out to the garden. When they were gone, Lacey looked over at Naomi and Shirley. "Help yourself to teas and coffees. And if you get hungry, Tom's just over the road. He'd be very happy to bake you some fresh croissants."

Naomi and Shirley both looked pleased with the compromise.

Satisfied that her family would be taken care of, Lacey hurried for the door, with Chester her trusty sidekick at her side, and a fire of determination burning in her belly to solve the case and save her wedding burning.

CHAPTER EIGHTEEN

"Hey, Ash," Lacey called across the Drawing Room to the mustachioed mixologist. "Can I ask you something?"

The Lodge's cocktail maker extraordinaire put down the glass he'd been polishing. "Fire away. This is about the murder, right? Totally crazy. The cops have been questioning everyone."

Lacey walked over to the wooden bar, Chester trotting along beside her. When she reached it, she leaned her arms on the dark mahogany wood.

"Before he died, I overheard the victim talking to someone over lunch," she explained. "I'm hoping to track that diner down."

Ash reached under the bar and brought out a binder. He flicked it open to reveal a diagram of the seating plan of the dining room. "Where were they sitting?"

"Greg, the victim, was here," Lacey said, pointing at the table by the kitchen doors. "The other diner was sitting on the next table over." She tapped the sketch to indicate the correct table.

"Table ten," Ash said. He flipped the page over to the corresponding list of bookings. "It was booked under *Moyles*." Then, with a tone of recognition, he added, "I wonder if it was Marcus?"

Lacey raised an eyebrow. "Marcus Moyles? That was his name?"

"Yeah," Ash said. "If it's the same Moyles who comes in here regularly, I mean."

"Describe him."

"Brown hair. Freckles. Fifty-odd."

Lacey nodded. The description matched the man she'd seen Greg bragging to about the gold over lunch. "That sounds like him. He's not a guest at the Lodge?"

Ash shook his head. "No. He's a local. Lives in Wollenton Green. But he comes in here all the time because, well, obviously I make the best cocktails." He grinned cheekily.

"Wollenton Green?" Lacey muttered, her chest sinking. That was the next town over. And since she'd been expressly forbidden from leaving Wilfordshire, that meant she couldn't go and interrogate her prime suspect. If Marcus Moyles had been a guest at the Lodge, she would've been able to question him here, but since he was outside of Wilfordshire he was totally out of her reach.

She looked back at Ash. "What are the chances he comes in tonight?"

"Pretty high," Ash replied. "He's quite the boozer." He mimed glugging a drink.

"He's an alcoholic?" Lacey questioned. Not that it made him any more guilty, but people could act irrationally when under the influence, and small fights could easily escalate into big ones.

Ash shrugged. "I'm not a doctor. I just make the cocktails. And let's just say he likes a lot of cocktails…"

"Will you give me a call if he comes in again tonight?" Lacey asked, filled with disappointment. It was cutting it fine, but even if she had to wait until the evening to question Marcus Moyles it still increased her chances of being able to go ahead with her original wedding plans.

"Sure," Ash said. "But why are you so interested in him?" Then he gasped and drew his brows in together. He lowered his voice to a whisper. "You don't think he's the killer, do you?"

Lacey paused as she considered just how much she should be involving Ash in the case. "I have a theory I want to test," she said.

Ash drew back. He looked troubled, so far from the cocky young man Lacey knew him to be. She shouldn't have told him anything.

"Just call me if he comes back. Please?" She handed him her business card so he'd have her number close at hand. Time in this case was very much of the essence.

Ash took it, scanning it with his eyes. "I—I, yeah. Sure. Of course." His gaze snapped up to hers. "But Lacey. Am I in danger or anything? Like, shouldn't I be calling the police if I see him instead of you?"

"Unless you happen to have a pocket full of antique gold, my guess is he won't be interested in you," Lacey said. "Beyond fixing him his martinis, of course."

Ash paused for a moment, then nodded. He seemed placated enough with that answer. He pocketed the business card and went back to polishing his glass.

"Come on, Chester," Lacey said. "Let's go."

Her dog followed her as she walked back across the dining room and headed through the corridor of the Lodge toward the exit. The atmosphere inside the inn felt a million miles away from its usual vibe. There was a heavy somberness in the air, so thick Lacey could almost feel it against her skin. It was as if Greg Ford's murder had made a dark rain cloud form over the inn.

As Lacey retraced her steps back through the Lodge and into the foyer, the name Marcus Moyles repeated over and over in her head. Could he be her guy? He was the only person right now with a motive for murder.

Her footsteps sounded on the slate tiles as she walked to the automatic glass doors. They swished open for her, and she stepped out into the bracing cold day.

She trotted down the external steps of the inn, Chester at her side, deliberating over whether she should just go to Wollenton Green anyway and question Marcus Moyles. It was risky. She could be spotted and thrown in a cell for her troubles. But what other option did she have? If he didn't come to the dining room to drink tonight, she'd fail anyway.

She reached the gravel lot and began walking toward her car. But as she went, she spotted a black car now parked beside her champagne Volvo that had not been there before. She recognized the tinted windows right away. The car was Superintendent Turner's…

Lacey felt a spike of anxiety. What was he doing here? Had he followed her?

She drew closer, her view widening, and spotted the detective leaning against his car, arms crossed, an expectant look in his eyes. His gaze was fixed on her. His unimpressed expression grew even stronger the closer she got.

Lacey swallowed, under no doubt now that he was waiting for her. Which meant he was keeping a close eye on her. But why? He'd made it clear she wasn't a suspect, so why was he watching her like a hawk?

Superintendent Turner pushed off the car as she reached him. "Lacey. I thought I might find you here. You came here to investigate the murder, I presume?"

"No," Lacey fibbed. "I'm just trying to make arrangements in case we have to postpone or change my wedding plans tomorrow. Which I'm guessing by the fact you're standing here and not interrogating your prime suspect is becoming a very real possibility…"

Superintendent Turner said nothing. Instead, a small smirk tugged at the side of his mouth.

"Speaking of your wedding—" he began.

Hope leapt in Lacey's chest. Had he had a change of heart? Would he give her permission to leave Wilfordshire after all?

"—did my invite get lost in the post?" he finished.

Lacey's chest sank, her hope dashed. He was mocking her. Rubbing it in. "You were expecting an invite? Really?"

Suddenly, Superintendent Turner's face cracked into laughter. "I'm joking!" he cried. "I know I'm not invited. Goodness, you should see your face!"

Lacey folded her arms. She was not impressed. "Can I get to my car, please?" she said. If Turner was going to go ahead with ruining her wedding, at the very least he could not force her to waste her time with awkward conversation as well.

"Of course," Turner said, stepping aside. "But aren't you just itching to tell me what you found?"

Lacey paused. She turned back and frowned at him. "What?"

"Inside," Turner said, jerking his head toward the inn. "You're here following a lead, aren't you? So? Don't you want to tell me what you found? You normally do."

Lacey narrowed her eyes. She was far from being in the right frame of mind for his taunts. "You're not usually open to my suggestions."

"You're not usually so coy about giving them to me."

Touché.

"I overheard Greg talking to another diner," Lacey admitted. "Shortly before he died."

Superintendent Turner looked interested. "Go on?"

"He was bragging about having found Jacobite gold. I thought that maybe he picked the wrong guy to brag about it to. Someone who saw it as an opportunity to steal."

"A burglary gone wrong scenario," Superintendent Turner offered.

Lacey shrugged. "It's a motive, isn't it? People have killed for less."

A spark in Superintendent Turner's eyes told Lacey she was onto something. He began nodding slowly, his eyes darting back and forth as he processed something internally.

"Yes," he said, meeting her gaze again. "Yes, it does." He sounded animated. "Did you get a name for this guy?"

Lacey could hardly believe this. Superintendent Karl Turner was actually listening to her for once. He was actually asking for her help. Just imagine how much they could've achieved had he listened to her all those other times in the past?

"Marcus Moyles," she said. "He's a regular. Lives in Wollenton Green."

Superintendent Turner jotted it down in his notebook. "That is helpful," he said, dotting the sentence with a flourish. He clicked the pen lid. "Very helpful indeed."

Lacey blinked at this newer, more chipper Superintendent Turner. For the first time, she could actually picture him as a younger man, a sharp, intelligent, eager detective. She wondered when he'd gotten so jaded. Why it had all gone awry for him along the way. And, more interestingly, how he seemed to be pulling it all back together once again. Maybe there was hope after all to fix her broken family…

"Aren't you going to ask?" Karl said suddenly, snapping her from her reverie.

"Ask what?"

"Ask why your statement is so helpful."

Lacey's inner sleuth was obviously desperate to know what she'd stumbled upon here. Superintendent Turner had clearly found a piece of evidence that her own theory matched up with. But she'd never expected him to actually voluntarily share it with her. She felt pride stirring in her chest.

"Yes. Yes, of course," she stammered, surprised.

"We have evidence," Superintendent Turner said, "that Greg Ford's hotel room door was tampered with." He smacked his notebook on his hand with triumph. "And this might very well tell us why."

Lacey paused as she absorbed the new piece of the puzzle. "His door was tampered with?" she echoed.

Superintendent Turner wiggled his brows. "Clear signs of an attempted break-in. We're pursuing a theft theory. This help builds up a clearer picture."

Lacey was astonished. Not just because she'd finally seemed to have won Superintendent Turner over, but because she was hopeful again that perhaps this case might be solved in time for her wedding to go ahead.

"So what now?" she asked the detective. "Interview Marcus Moyles?"

Superintendent Turner tucked his notebook back away in the breast pocket of his beige trench coat. "That's right." He fixed his eyes on Lacey, and used a tone of warning. "*I* interview Marcus Moyles. Me and Lewis. Not YOU. And definitely not Fido."

From where he was waiting beside her, Chester let out a low, grumpy whine. Lacey's earlier moment of happiness ebbed away.

Turner was still determined to keep her at arm's length, even if he had conceded she was useful to the case.

"Do you understand?" he added. "I'll be taking it from here. You go back to your store and do whatever it is you do. Sell some antiques."

Lacey twisted her lips in consideration. She was only investigating because of the threat to her wedding. But if she'd successfully pointed the detectives in the direction of the prime suspect, maybe if she butted out and let him do his job now, everything would be okay in the end after all.

Karl Turner leaned against the cruiser again, waiting expectantly for her confirmation.

Lacey nodded. "Fine. I'll leave it."

"Thank you," he said, visibly exhaling his relief.

Lacey headed for the car.

"Oh, and Lacey?" Karl called to her from behind.

She looked back. "Yes?"

"You can take your monk back."

"My monk?"

"Brother Benedict. We've finished questioning him. Released an hour ago."

Lacey's mouth fell open. "You mean… you thought he was a suspect?" So much for keeping out of Superintendent Turner's cases, it seemed like the moment she turned her back he went and didn't something stupid like questioning a monk!

"Of course we did. He might be a holy man now, but one look into his background tells a different story. Petty crime. Drugs. It's all there. All the hallmarks of a future killer."

Lacey remembered what Abbot Weeks had told her about Brother Benedict when they'd first met. He'd been an at-risk youth, the very type the monastery was aiming to help. But he was quite clearly reformed. He'd taken a vow of pacifism.

"We had witness reports saying he would hang around the bandstand for hours at peculiar times of the day. Add that to the report from the attempted robbery at your store, where he was on site during it yet apparently heard nothing, you can see how it built up a picture." Then he chuckled and shook his head. "Just turns out he's very committed to meditation. Can block out the entire world. I've never seen anything like it in my life!"

At the mention of his meditation habits, Lacey pictured the way he'd hover silently in the corner of her office.

"Wait," she said with a sudden thought. "He's in the middle of a silent holy prayer. How did you get him to speak?"

"We didn't at first. Took a call to the head abbot to convince him the big guy upstairs wouldn't be offended on this one occasion."

Lacey grimaced at the thought of Abbot Weeks receiving a call from the Wilfordshire police. He'd sent the monk with her to protect the scepter, and she'd gotten him embroiled in a murder case. She suspected he would have something to say about that, once she made it back to the store.

"Anyway," Turner added, "he's gone back to being silent again now. Reset the clock, too, I reckon. Another ten days. Poor bugger. Oh look, there he is now."

Lacey looked over to see the monk coming down the steps of the Lodge. She couldn't imagine him talking, she was so used to his silent mannerisms, but she imagined he'd have a very calm, soothing voice.

As he walked toward her, Lacey tried to picture him as the troubled youth he'd once been, as a man capable of violence. There was nothing in him anymore that even hinted at the person he'd been before. He was calm. Tranquil. At peace. The monastery's program had saved him, and Lacey's desire to value and sell the scepter to keep St. Cyril's operating reared back to life. She'd gotten sidetracked by the murder case for selfish reasons. But there were greater and more important things to focus on than herself. Saving St. Cyril's troubled teens program.

Brother Benedict reached her and smiled.

"Shall we get back to the shop?" Lacey said. "And get to work? I have a bunch of interesting papers to read through."

Brother Benedict bowed his agreement.

Lacey turned to Superintendent Turner to say farewell. But before she spoke, it occurred to her this may very well be the last time she ever saw him. If she was right about Marcus Moyles, and the case was closed, Superintendent Turner would retire and their paths would never cross again. She felt a strange pang of nostalgia for the man with whom she'd shared a fraught and at times antagonist relationship.

"Good bye, Karl," she said.

"Hope I don't see you, kid," he replied.

Lacey turned away and headed to the car, confident that the investigation was in good hands. She had more important things to focus on, like the scepter. She felt more eager than ever to get on with the work so St. Cyril's could continue all their good work in turn.

With Brother Benedict strapped in the passenger seat beside her, Lacey gunned her car to life and backed out of the space. She actually felt optimistic for what felt like the first time in days.

But as she drove back to the high street, her optimism popped like a balloon. Because as she passed by her store and glanced through the window, she spotted two people inside. Two people who should never be seen together.

It was her mom and dad.

CHAPTER NINETEEN

"Quick, quick, quick!" Lacey cried to Brother Benedict as she hurriedly parked in the side alley and threw her car door open.

Brother Benedict looked flustered as he gathered up his robes and fumbled with the handle on the passenger side.

"I'm sorry to rush you," Lacey said, jumping out of the car. "But if we don't get to my store now some seriously unholy stuff will go down!"

The monk frowned with confusion. He slid out the passenger side, Chester following after him, and slammed the door shut. Lacey closed hers too and locked up, then raced as fast as her legs could take her to her store.

Her heart was pounding as she shoved open the door and burst inside. It took a split second to confirm that she'd entered into a scene of utter chaos.

"This is all your fault!" Shirley was screaming.

"My fault?" Frank screamed back. "How is it my fault?"

"You've manipulated her, haven't you? Told her to change all the plans I made! You've swanned back into her life after all these years and filled her head with nonsense ideas!"

Lacey's heart seized with panic, even while she frowned with complete confusion at whatever it was they were talking about. She felt like a seven-year-old all over again, her eyes darting back and forth between her parents just as they had done back in NYC before her father finally stormed out of the house for the very last time. And just like when she was a child, she was at a complete loss as to what her parents were screaming about.

Just then, she spotted Gina standing by the counter. The older woman was standing mouth agape, staring at Shirley and Frank with a panicked and worried expression. Deducing if anyone knew what was going on here, it would be her, Lacey hurried to her friend. Her monk and dog followed behind her.

"Gina! What's going on?"

Gina flinched with surprise and turned to face her. "Oh, Lacey! You're here."

Lacey knew Gina too well; she was feeling guilty about something, it was written all over her face.

Lacey put her hands on her hips. "Yes. I'm here. And I'm wondering what on earth is going on." She threw her arm toward her warring parents.

Gina wrung her hands nervously. "I might have… accidentally… let slip to Shirley that there was a possibility of a venue change tomorrow…"

Lacey winced. Shirley had been the one who'd found the forest location in the first place. She must've jumped to conclusions when she heard there was a possible last-minute change, and assumed Frank had been the one to instigate it. Which of course was not the truth at all, but when had her mother let a pesky little thing like the truth hold her back from lashing out?

"She thinks my dad manipulated me into changing it?" Lacey stated.

"Sounds that way," Gina replied with a nervous nod.

Lacey ground her teeth. It was bad enough that she may have to change venues in the first place. But having her parents use it as an excuse to fight like cats and dogs was even worse.

She steeled herself and stepped forward to intervene.

"Stop!" she shouted as she marched across the floorboards toward them. "There's been a huge misunderstanding!"

But her parents didn't even notice her.

"You want the wedding on the cliffs, don't you?" Shirley screamed. "Those damn cliffs you love so much!"

"The location of the ceremony isn't important to me!" Frank screamed back.

"Oh, that's rich coming from you, mister!" Shirley screamed. Her pointer finger was out again, and she was waggling it right in Frank's face. "You left your entire family for those stupid cliffs once! If you can do *THAT* then you can do *THIS* too!"

Lacey stood there, her eyes going back and forth between her parents as she watched their tennis match of a fight unfold. She felt helpless. The only saving grace was that Naomi and Frankie weren't here to witness it—they must've headed out to get some breakfast.

As Lacey stood there trying to work out what to do or say to break the two apart, the door suddenly opened with a tinkle. She looked over to see Taryn came trotting in.

Not now, Lacey thought desperately. This was the last thing she needed.

"Oh, Lacey!" Taryn gushed, apparently oblivious to her incredibly bad timing.

At the sight of his own personal Cruella De Vil, Chester started to growl. Boudica caught on and growled too. The sound of the growling dogs only added to the cacophony of noise swirling around Lacey. She clenched her teeth.

Taryn gave the dogs a dirty look as she sidestepped them and grasped Lacey's arm in her hand. "I heard about the murder," she said, dramatically, her bony fingers digging in to Lacey's flesh. "How awful!"

Lacey tried to shake her off. "Yes," she said between her tightly clenched teeth. "It's terrible."

"And right before your wedding," Taryn continued.

She was using her syrupy voice, the one she used when she was actually giving out back-handed compliments. It didn't take a genius to work out that she was actually reveling in the thought of the murder overshadowing her wedding. She had no concern for the victim whatsoever. All she cared about was the fact that Lacey wouldn't be getting her perfect wedding anymore.

"You must be devastated," Taryn continued, her fingers like talons on Lacey's arm. "Are you okay?"

With the backdrop of her parents' screaming match and the growling dogs, Lacey swirled to face Taryn and wrenched her arm free.

"Do I look okay?!" she yelled.

All at once, silence fell. Shirley and Frank paused and looked at Lacey with shock. Gina's eyes widened. Brother Benedict blinked with surprise. Even Boudica and Chester stared at her.

But Lacey didn't care. She'd snapped. She'd been holding too much in over the last few days and now it was all coming out.

Taryn took a step backward, looking stunned, almost as if Lacey had slapped her.

"Well?" Lacey demanded. "Do I? Since you're suddenly so concerned about my well-being, after months and months of being nothing but cruel to me! Do you really want to know how I am, or do you just think that by being nice to me now you can get you an invite to my wedding?"

Taryn's face fell. She looked humiliated that her attempts to win Lacey over had been so transparent.

"What are you talking about?" she replied, feigning disinterest. "Why would I want to go to your wedding?"

"My thoughts exactly," Lacey cried. "You obviously hate me. I can only assume you want to come to ruin it!"

Taryn stuck out her bottom lip into a pout. "Narcissistic much?" she sneered. "I have much more important things to think about than your poxy wedding." And with that, she turned on her spindly heel and marched back out the way she'd come.

Lacey took a deep, ragged breath, needing a moment to calm her frayed nerves. When she glanced up, she saw all eyes were on her. She must look like a crazy person to them. From their perspective, she'd just blown up at a perfectly nice person asking a perfectly reasonable question.

"I really need you guys to leave," Lacey said, in the calmest voice she could muster. She didn't trust herself now. If she could blow up like that at Taryn, she could blow up at her parents. She didn't want to say something she would later come to regret.

Frank stepped forward. "Lacey love, what's—"

"—No!" Lacey barked, holding her hand up to stop him. Not because she didn't want her father's support right now, but because she knew it would only stoke her mother's flames once again. "Just go."

Frank halted. Then he stepped back again. Shirley looked smug that Lacey had rejected him.

Just then, the door opened again, and this time Tom entered.

"Guys! What is going on in here?" he demanded. He glanced from one tense face to the next. "I can hear the shouting from the other side of the street!"

No one said a word. The awkwardness was overwhelming.

"Nothing," Lacey stammered. "Everyone was just leaving. Mom. Dad. Please, just go."

Shirley looked at Tom. "Frank has changed the wedding venue," she said, haughtily.

"And Shirley won't believe that I had nothing to do with it!" Frank countered. "Why don't you tell her? Maybe she'll listen to you."

Lacey's shoulders sank as Tom blanched with astonishment. His head darted toward Lacey. There was a deep furrow of confusion on his brow.

"What's happened to the wedding?" he asked in a pained voice.

Lacey's stomach dropped. This wasn't how she'd wanted to do it, but now she had no choice. "We might not be able to have the ceremony in the forest anymore," she said, sadly.

"Why?" Tom asked. He sounded aghast. Lacey felt terrible for all the trouble she'd caused. "Because Superintendent Turner has forbidden me from leaving town during the investigation," she admitted.

Tom blinked. His expression was unreadable. "You're not a suspect."

She shook her head. "No. But Karl's retiring and he doesn't want me messing up his last case."

Tom looked shell-shocked. He sank down into the red velvet love seat. "Oh," was all he said.

Lacey chewed her lip fretfully. *Oh* wasn't a lot to go on. What was he really thinking?

"Wait," Shirley said in the silence. "*That's* why the venue changed?"

"Yes," Lacey said. "It has nothing to do with Dad, and everything to do with my long history of meddling in cases when I shouldn't."

Everyone looked at her. She couldn't tell if they were disappointed in her, but she certainly felt like they were. At the very least, she was disappointed in herself.

Tom stood again and paced to Lacey. He took her gently by the shoulders. "Look, Lacey. It's okay. I don't mind where I marry you, just as long as I do. Can the reception still go ahead?"

She nodded. "The Drawing Room is safe territory. No change there."

"So then it's just a matter of organizing a location switch for the ceremony, right?"

Lacey nodded. Tom seemed to have gone into pragmatic mode, she noted with relief. If anyone could talk her off the ledge, it was him.

"Then that's what we'll do," he said, smiling at her gently, encouragingly. "There's no disaster here. Just a last-minute change in plans. And when it comes to us, that's always to be expected, right?"

Lacey let out a small chuckle. As sad as she was, Tom's words had greatly comforted her. He was right. They'd weathered worse storms.

"Where shall we change it to?" Lacey asked.

"Where do you want?" Tom replied, taking both her hands in his.

Lacey thought about all the beautiful places in Wilfordshire, from the hillsides to the beautiful old pub. But there was one place more perfect than any other.

"The beach," she said. "By the cliffs."

Shirley threw her hands up in despair and muttered something about, *"On a beach! In winter!"* but Lacey wasn't focusing on her. She was too busy gazing into Tom's green eyes.

"The beach it is," he said, tenderly.

Lacey leaned onto her tiptoes and kissed him, filled with love, appreciation, and gratitude. All that stress and worry, she should've known to offload it all to Tom, that he'd be able to take it in his stride and make everything okay. He would've married her in The Cod Father, their local chippy, if that was what she wanted.

Tom looked over at Gina. "Can you call the officiary and sort out the change in location?" he said. Then he looked at Frank. "Frank, I need you to make sure all the guests are aware of the change. The contact numbers are on the list, so it's just a case of calling everyone." He looked at Shirley. "You arranged the harpist, right? See if she can still play on the beach. If not, we can have her play at the Drawing Room before the bluegrass band. Okay?"

All three of them nodded quickly, taking their orders.

Then Tom turned to Lacey. "Now. You're coming with me."

"What? Where are we going? I have work to do."

He took her hand. "Not for the next hour you don't. I'm taking you to lunch."

He whisked her toward the exit. Lacey looked helplessly back at Brother Benedict. She was supposed to be doing work on the scepter. The monk smiled gently and held up a hand as if in reassurance, but Lacey wasn't convinced.

"Tom, I don't have time for lunch," she said. "I have work to do."

But as they reached the door, Tom turned to look at her. "You have no choice," he said seriously. "We have something very important to discuss."

Lacey's stomach tightened. She did not like the sound of that. Her mind turned over all the possibilities of what exactly he needed to discuss. Had he somehow found out about her pregnancy scare? Was he upset with her?

She chewed her lip. There was only one way to find out. She relented, letting Tom whisk her out of the store by the hand.

CHAPTER TWENTY

Lacey sank wearily into the chair across the bistro table opposite Tom and rubbed the tension from between her eyebrows. She was starting to get a headache—partly from her parents shouting, and partly from the anxiety over what exactly the important thing was that Tom needed to discuss.

Chester slunk under the table, settling down on her feet like a warm, weighted blanket. She appreciated the comfort.

The café Tom had taken her to was a cute Parisian-style coffee shop, a little off the beaten track, with low lighting and marble-topped tables. The delicate smells of sweet French desserts permeated the air, and the tinkle of crockery provided a gentle background white noise.

Tom leaned across the table and took Lacey's hands in his. "Tell me what's going on with you," he said.

Lacey took a deep breath. Tom's green eyes were gentle and reassuring. So he didn't know? He wasn't here to grill her? He just wanted to talk?

She felt her defenses start to weaken. "I don't know where to begin," she admitted.

"Start with the ceremony," he said, softly. "Why didn't you tell me Superintendent Turner had essentially forbidden you from going to your own wedding?"

He was speaking without anger, without malice, and his overwhelming reassurance made Lacey feel suddenly ridiculous for having kept the whole wedding troubles from him in the first place.

"I don't know. Because of the omen? Because I thought you'd disapprove? Because I thought if I solved the case before tomorrow, you'd never even need to find out?"

Tom tutted affectionately and shook his head. "You can't help yourself when it comes to sleuthing, can you?" he said. But it was without judgment. Tom had expressed his concerns with how deeply Lacey threw herself into police matters before, yet he had clearly accepted this part of her, or he wouldn't be sitting opposite her now, one day away from committing to her for the rest of his life, and not looking even remotely like he was about to run for the hills.

Lacey shook her head, sighing at herself for her silly behavior. "I'm sorry."

"Don't be," Tom said. "I'm not trying to make you feel guilty. I just don't like it when you keep secrets from me."

Lacey opened her mouth to speak, but shut it again, as her mind wandered to the other secret she'd been keeping from Tom. The pregnancy scare. She had to tell him.

Mustering up the courage, Lacey opened her mouth to explain. But before she uttered the first syllable, Tom's gaze suddenly went past her shoulder.

"Harry?" he cried.

Surprised, Lacey turned in her chair. Tom's distant ex-step-half-cousin was halfway through the café door, his bright yellow sports car parked on the cobblestone curb just beyond.

"Tom!" Harry cried, looking just as surprised to have run into him. He took Tom's extended hand and pulled him into an embrace, laughing merrily.

"What are you doing here?" Tom said.

"Just checking out the competition," he said with another chuckle. "I want to see whose macarons are the best."

Tom let out a hearty belly laugh. Lacey was pleased to see how happy he was in Harry's company, and felt guilty that she didn't share the sentiment.

Harry turned to her. "Lacey!" he said, genially.

He bent down and bestowed kisses on each of her cheeks. She raised herself slightly to accept them, but didn't stand all the way.

"Sit down!" Tom cried, enthusiastically. "Join us for lunch. That's okay, isn't it, Lacey?"

Stomach sinking, Lacey had no choice but to nod. "Yes. Of course. The more the merrier."

So much for no more secrets.

*

"Lochaber," Harry said, leaning forward to dunk his bread roll in the small dish of olive oil. "Beautiful place to live." He took a big bite of his bread and looked at Lacey as he spoke through his mouthful. "You ever been to Scotland, Lace?"

Lacey cringed at the sound of the nickname she disliked so much. She prodded her barely eaten salad with her fork and shook her head. Tiger prawn linguine salad with a chili and lime dressing had all the hallmarks of being her favorite, but she'd lost her appetite for it.

Harry tutted at Tom. "What's wrong with you?" he ribbed. "Not taking your lovely lady to the most beautiful place in the UK!" He looked at Lacey and wiggled his brows. "You know there's still time to change your mind and marry me," he joked.

Tom laughed, but Lacey was barely able to rouse a smile. As wonderful as it was having his distant second cousin here for Tom, it was actually a bit of an imposition for Lacey. She was not in the right headspace to entertain him, and he always seemed to be there at just the wrong moment.

"Harry works in excavation," Tom informed her.

"Oh?" Lacey said, politely.

"Dredging lochs," Harry replied. "It's not glamorous, but it makes me a decent enough wage."

He pointed again to the yellow sports car out the window. He was obviously very proud of it. Lacey was starting to find his bragging a little bit grating.

"How's your business, Lacey?" Harry asked. "Tom's told me everything there is to know about pastry." He pretended to yawn. "But I'm more interested in what you do. Antiques. Auctioneering. I bet you've sold some really fascinating treasures in your time."

"Uh-huh," Lacey said absentmindedly, prodding a prawn on her plate with her fork. "Sculptures. Jewels. Art. A Roman coin. It's all been very exciting."

"Sounds great," Harry said, leaning forward on his elbows with interest, as if wanting more.

Lacey shifted uncomfortably. She had nothing more to offer. Her heart really wasn't in this conversation. Her mind was too full of all kinds of other worries to chat about her job.

"Tell me," Harry said, prompting her since she wasn't being forthcoming. "What's the most expensive thing you've ever sold?" His eyes flashed with interest.

Lacey took a moment to think about it. The most expensive item had been a letter from Queen Victoria to Charles Dickens, but that had turned out to be a forgery and the payment reversed, so probably didn't count.

"I guess it was when—" Lacey began, but her voice trailed away as her gaze was caught by someone walking past the window.

Brown hair. Freckles. Fifty-odd.

It was Marcus Moyles!

She jumped up from her seat, catching her knife and fork as she did and making them clatter loudly against the side of the ceramic dish. Her sudden movement made Tom and Harry jump with surprise. From beneath the table, Chester leapt to attention and scrambled out, his ears pointing upward, alert.

"Lacey?" Tom said, looking surprised. "Are you okay?"

Lacey kept her eyes on Marcus Moyles walking by the window as she replied. "I'm fine. I have something to do. I'll be right back." She discarded her napkin on the table.

"Lacey!" Tom exclaimed, standing as she dashed for the door. He looked bemused at her suddenly running out on lunch. "Where are you going?"

Lacey paused, hand on the door handle. She felt bad about running out, but she suddenly had a shot at solving the case. She might've promised the detectives not to meddle, but this opportunity had simply dropped in her lap, and she'd be a fool not to take it.

"I'll be right back!" she cried, heaving open the door.

And with that, she dashed out of the café on the tail of Marcus Moyles, leaving a stunned-looking Tom and Harry behind.

CHAPTER TWENTY ONE

"Marcus!" Lacey cried as she raced along the street to catch up to her prime suspect. "Marcus Moyles!"

At the sound of his name, the man halted. He turned, took one look at the woman barreling down the street after him with an English shepherd at her heels, then turned back around and broke into a sprint.

"Oh no you don't, you slimy weasel," Lacey said.

She took off after him.

Marcus raced along the cobblestones, turning at a small side alleyway and disappearing out of sight. Lacey raced after him onto the small pedestrianized footpath flanked by tall town houses either side. As they went, Marcus kept making furtive, panicked glances behind him.

"Stop!" Lacey called, but of course he did not listen.

Heart pumping, Lacey followed Marcus and saw him dart through the wrought iron gates of the public gardens. The small patch of grass was popular with locals, especially young families and dog walkers, and was full of overgrown hedges. He wasn't going to attempt to hide, was he? Lacey wondered.

She raced through the gate after him, propelling herself so quickly its hinges creaked in protest. The green was filled with buggies and prams, and small children in puffy winter jackets crisscrossing on their push scooters. Lacey suddenly realized why Marcus had chosen to divert this way. Not to hide, but because of all the moving obstacles now blocking her from him.

She screeched to a halt, narrowly avoiding slamming straight into a small child on a tricycle, and craned her neck with frustration as Marcus dodged and weaved through a group of chilly-looking picnickers, beelining for the exit gate on the other side.

"Chester," Lacey said, turning to her dog. "It's over to you, buddy. Bring him down."

Chester immediately obeyed. He went racing across the gardens, weaving around the children on their various modes of transport, leaping over babies in prams, jumping from one bench to the next, much to the astonishment of the young women sitting on them sipping coffee, then leapt through the air, paws first, and rammed Marcus Moyles square in the back.

Marcus staggered, then went down to his knees. Chester shoved his paws on his shoulders and the man folded forward. Chester, the victor, barked with triumph.

Lacey punched the air. "Good boy!" she cried.

But when she realized everyone was staring at her aghast, she felt the need to shake an apologetic hand. "Don't worry. Citizen's arrest," she said, coyly.

She hurried through the gardens, passing all the stunned children and astonished picnickers who just moments earlier had been used as a stepping-stone for an English shepherd, and reached the crumpled form of Marcus Moyles.

"Aha!" she exclaimed, bending down and turning the man around.

She held him by the lapels of his suit. His clothes were rumpled from when Chester had rugby-tackled him to the ground. There was dirt smudged across his chin.

"Why are you chasing me?" he cried, sounding terrified.

"Because you're a criminal!" Lacey accused. "I know what you did at the Lodge. Admit it!"

The crowd of onlookers were all murmuring between themselves now. Several people had stood up to get a better view. Several more were on their cell phones, no doubt calling the cops. *Little did they know,* Lacey thought triumphantly.

"What are you talking about?" Marcus cried.

"Don't play dumb with me," Lacey said, giving him a little shake for emphasis. "I was there in the dining room the day Greg was murdered. I overheard him bragging to you about the gold he'd found. You stole it off him, didn't you!"

Suddenly, tears welled in Marcus's eyes. "I was drunk!"

"You think that's an excuse?" she demanded.

"No," he stammered. "No. I know it's not an excuse. But it's the truth. I drank too much. I lost my judgment. My sense of morality."

Lacey couldn't quite believe she'd gotten a confession out of him so easily. And with so many witnesses. But then she realized he'd not said the confession aloud, and it would count for nothing unless he did.

"So you admit it?" she prompted, pressing him by the lapels against the ground in what she hoped was a vaguely intimidating way.

"Yes! Yes! I admit it! I broke into his room. I tried to steal his gold."

"And then what? He caught you? You fought?" She shook him again. "How did it go from attempted burglary to murder?"

Marcus paused. He blinked at her, looking perplexed. He took a few moments to register what she had just accused him of, before his whole demeanor shifted dramatically.

"Murder?" he echoed incredulously. "You think I killed him? I did nothing of the sort!" He tried to shove her hands off, but failed. "I tried to steal his gold, that's all."

"A likely story," Lacey said, tightening her grip on his lapels. But doubt was starting to form in her mind. The change in his mannerisms had been quite abrupt when she'd accused him of murder, and not the sort of thing that could easily be faked. She shook the doubts away. All signs had led to Marcus. Besides, only guilty men ran. "If you didn't kill him, then why did you run the moment you saw me?"

"Because of your dog!" Marcus stammered. "And because of…" His eyes suddenly widened at something over her shoulder. "…Him!"

Lacey swirled. A huge hulking figure was looming above them. She held her arm up to shield her eyes from the bright winter sun, only to find herself staring up into the furious eyes of Superintendent Turner.

Her stomach clenched. "Uh-oh."

"Lacey, please get off this man," Superintendent Turner said calmly.

He had his hands on his hips, and his face was blank. Not that Lacey was fooled. She knew Karl Turner well enough now to know he was fuming, he just had an amazing ability to remain measured.

With a grimace, Lacey rolled off of Marcus Moyles and stood.

Chester followed her lead, leaving the crumpled figure now entirely exposed. He had his hands up in a truce position, with a terrified look on his face. He looked rather pathetic lying there, Lacey couldn't help but think.

Superintendent Turner bent down and offered him a hand to help him up. Cautiously, Marcus took the detective's hand and allowed himself to be tugged to his feet—something the largely built Superintendent Turner managed with ease. Once standing, he smoothed down his rumpled clothes.

"Marcus Moyles?" Superintendent Turner asked.

"That's right," the trembling man replied.

"I'm arresting you on suspicion of breaking and entering." The detective produced cuffs from his pocket. "It's in relation to an attempted theft at the Lodge hotel."

Marcus's gaze dropped to his feet with shame. Superintendent Turner continued reading him his rights as he cuffed his hands behind his back and led him to the waiting car on the other side of the iron gates.

As they went, Lacey spotted DCI Lewis coming in through the gates. She came right up to her and folded her arms sternly.

"Is this what not getting involved looks like to you?" she asked with dry sarcasm. "You promised to leave this case alone!"

"Our prime suspect walked right past my window," Lacey explained. "I couldn't exactly sit there and do nothing!"

Beth was shaking her head. "Our? *Our?* Lacey! You're not a cop! Marcus Moyles is mine and Karl's prime suspect and he's nothing to do with you whatsoever."

"Aha!" Lacey exclaimed. "You admit he's your prime suspect." She felt vindicated. As much as she disliked being admonished by her friend, it did take the sting out of it somewhat when she knew she was in the right.

Beth puckered her lips. "Yes. Okay. He is a prime suspect. But we were already on his tail. You didn't need to get involved."

"Well, I didn't know that, did I?" Lacey continued. "For all I knew, he might well have been a flight risk."

"Flight risk or not, it's not your job," Beth continued.

Lacey just couldn't agree. She'd prefer to get in trouble for something she'd done, than to do nothing and have someone else end up dead! The ends certainly justified the means, as far as she was concerned.

"Well, I'm sorry to have been such an inconvenience to you," Lacey replied.

Beth rolled her eyes. "Your dog pounced on him," she continued. "You know it's against the law to have a dangerously out of control dog."

"Now you and I both know Chester is neither dangerous nor out of control," Lacey replied, petting her patiently waiting pooch. "And I personally think his takedown was rather elegant. Besides, it was at my command anyway and—"

"Lacey!" Beth snapped, losing her patience. "These witnesses don't know that." She threw her arm out to the passerby in the park, many of whom had already lost interest in the ruckus and gone back to whatever they'd been doing in the first place. "As far as they're concerned, some crazed dog just pounced on a member of the public for no reason. They're probably expecting me to impound him for their safety!"

Lacey looked over at Chester, sitting alert beside her. He barked happily. He must be very proud of his efforts. As he should be. As far as Lacey was concerned, they'd caught the bad guy. The cops should be thanking them, not threatening impoundment! Especially when anyone with two eyes could see he wouldn't so much as hurt a fly, and none of the people around them seemed to care much about what had happened anyway.

"Why can't you just leave this alone?" Beth continued. "You're getting married tomorrow! Why don't you go home and relax or go to a spa or something. Jeez, Lacey."

"You know very well Karl basically left me no choice," Lacey explained. "He's ruining my wedding. My family is scrambling to get a plan B together as we speak."

"At least there is a plan B!" Beth snapped. "Because unless you stop meddling, you'll be spending your wedding day locked in a cell."

"Why is he being like this?" Lacey cried, gesturing to Superintendent Turner over by the car. "Why won't he let me bend this one rule?"

"One rule?" Beth repeated with raised eyebrows. "You have no idea how much flack that man's taken because of you. How many rules he's already bent for you. You think I'm the good guy on your side, and he's the bad guy against you? Who do you think let all those transgressions slide?"

Lacey snapped her lips together. It had never occurred to her that Karl Turner had been the one to pull all those strings to keep her out of jail—and there had been many, many times she'd done things she could've been arrested for. The thought that he had been defending her all this time made her feel awful for all the trouble she'd caused.

"I had no idea," Lacey said, lamely, her shame growing. "I'm sorry."

Beth sighed. "You're good at solving crimes, Lacey. If you were a detective, you'd be an asset. But you're a civilian. You put us in a difficult position every time you get involved. So we have no choice but to put our foot down this time. His retirement comes first." She pointed at Karl Turner standing by the Merc busy filling in the arrest form for Marcus Moyles. "I know we're friends, Lacey, but when it comes to your wedding versus his retirement and my promotion, you can see why there's too much at stake."

Lacey took a deep breath. She was defeated. There was no changing either of their minds on this one. No way to bend any of the rules. She had to stay out of the case and accept the reality that it wasn't going to get solved in time to save her forest ceremony. And if she didn't buck up and accept Plan B, there wouldn't be a wedding at all. Because she'd be sitting in a cell instead.

"I'm so sorry," Lacey said, sadly, seeing Beth's point of view. "I promise to stop."

CHAPTER TWENTY TWO

Lacey was about to head back to the café when she heard her phone ding with an incoming message. She checked it. It was from Tom.

Harry and I have left now. Hope everything's okay with you?

She cringed as she remembered running out on them. Harry probably thought she was very rude, and she would've liked the opportunity to go back and explain herself to him. But there was no chance now.

And worse than that, she'd lost her one chance of telling Tom about the pregnancy scare.

Shoulders slumped, she trudged back to the store instead.

She'd expected to at least have felt slightly happy to have caught Marcus and gotten a half confession out of him, but instead she felt disappointed that her efforts were going unnoticed.

The bell tinkled softly overhead as she went inside the store. To her surprise, it was now quiet and peaceful. She closed the door quietly behind her.

Chester hurried over to Boudica, wagging his tail as if to say, "You won't believe what just happened!"

Gina glanced up from the counter at Lacey standing by the door. She looked stressed. Harried. Lacey wondered what was going on.

"Where is everyone?" she asked, as she began walking across the shop floor toward her friend.

"Reorganizing your wedding!" Gina replied.

So that's why she looked so stressed, Lacey realized. She felt bad for her. This was a lot of pressure to take, changing everything last minute. Maybe it would be better just to call the whole thing off? At least then she could avoid her mom and dad meeting again and having another horrible repetition of the fight from earlier.

"Oh," Lacey said glumly. She reached the red velvet loveseat and flopped into it.

"You look terrible," Gina commented. "What's wrong?"

Lacey let her head drop into her hands, her dark curls falling over her arms. "Everything. My parents. The wedding." She looked up at her friend. "And I think I might be pregnant."

She hadn't meant to say it, but it just slipped out. Lacey had to admit, now that it was out there, it felt good to get a weight off her mind.

Gina's eyes widened with astonishment. "Oh darling, why didn't you say!" she exclaimed.

She hurried from around the counter and raced over to the loveseat, flopping down beside Lacey and cradling her in her arms in the sort of affectionate, motherly gesture Lacey's own mom rarely gave.

"How long have you been carrying that around on your own?" Gina cooed, gently.

"A couple days."

"Does Tom know?"

Lacey shook her head. "I keep meaning to tell him but it's never the right time. The first test was inconclusive. I thought if I took a second one and it was negative, I could just not tell him at all."

Gina released her and rolled her eyes, though it was without malice. "That's never sensible in a partnership, is it? You should tell each other everything."

"I know," Lacey said glumly. "But now his cousin Harry is here, there isn't any time. I tried to tell him over lunch but all Harry wanted to talk about was business." She sighed.

"Ugh, Cousin Harry," Gina said. She scoffed from the back of her throat.

"Not a fan?" Lacey asked.

Gina started to chuckle. In a low voice, she said, "Well, he's a bit bloody smarmy, isn't he?"

Lacey laughed. "I'm glad I'm not the only one who thinks so!"

She hated to admit it, since Tom seemed so thrilled his old buddy had turned up, but Harry just wasn't her cup of tea. He bragged a bit too much.

Just then, the store phone started to ring.

"I'd better get that," Lacey said with an exhalation. She pushed up from the couch and looked back down at Gina. "Thank you," she said to her friend. "For everything. I appreciate everything you've done for me."

"It's what friends are for," Gina replied with a smile. "Now pick up that phone before the ringing drives me batty."

Lacey smiled affectionately and went over to the counter. She picked up the phone. "Hello?"

"Lacey?" a croaky voice came on the other end, immediately recognizable as that of Abbot Weeks.

"Abbot Weeks," she said, surprised. "Is everything okay?"

"I've heard about what's going on there," the man replied. "Brother Benedict was questioned by the police? And was forced to break his prayerful silence?"

"Um… yes…" Lacey began. "I mean, it was an obvious misunderstanding and—"

"—I'm not happy about it," the abbot said, cutting her off. "I sent Brother Benedict with you because I had assumed this would be a safe project for him to oversee. That it would fit in well with his other commitments. Evidently, I have made a mistake. I want him to come back to the abbey. Now."

"Oh!" Lacey squeaked, her heart hitching. She'd grown very fond of Brother Benedict during his stay. He was a calming presence when it felt like everything else around her was descending into chaos. She'd be sorry to see him go. "I understand," she said into the receiver. "When can I expect his replacement to arrive?"

"Replacement?" Abbot Weeks exclaimed. "I'm not sending a replacement. I want Brother Benedict to come back and bring the scepter with him!"

Lacey's heart began to pound. "But—" she stammered. "But I've not finished my research yet."

"We'll have to get someone else to do the work," Abbot Weeks replied.

Lacey's shoulders slumped. She felt terrible. She'd really wanted to be the one to finish the job and help the charity she now strongly believed in. Instead, she'd let everyone down.

"I… I understand," she said, glumly. "I'll just go and fetch him."

But just as she was about to rest the phone down and head to the back room, the store door suddenly flew open. It was so abrupt and fast, the bell jangled noisily.

Startled, Lacey looked over to see a man come bounding in, wrapped up in a gray duffle coat with a Hufflepuff yellow and black striped scarf. It was Professor Crispin Noble, and he looked extremely excited.

Lacey cupped her hand over the phone's speaker. "Professor?" she asked as he hop-skipped toward her. "What's happened? Did you find something?"

"I think I did!" he cried. "I think I've cracked it!"

Hope blossomed in Lacey's chest. She removed her hand from over the speaker and spoke into it. "Abbot Weeks, can you give me just one last chance with the scepter? I think I might have had a breakthrough."

"It's too late," Abbot Weeks's voice croaked in her ear. "I've given you plenty of time."

Lacey squeezed the phone tightly, her gaze fixed on the eager face of Crispin Noble. "Please," she said. "Just a couple more hours. Then I'll drive Brother Benedict and the scepter back to the abbey myself, with the results."

There was a long pause. Finally, she heard the head abbot sigh.

"All right," he replied. "Everyone deserves a second chance."

"Thank you!" Lacey squeaked. "I won't let you down!"

She put down the phone.

Filled with anticipation, Lacey led Crispin Noble into the back room.

As they entered, Brother Benedict stirred from his position in the corner. A flash of curiosity registered in his eyes as he looked from Lacey to the professor.

"Good news," Lacey told him, enthused. "We might have had a breakthrough. And just in the nick of time. Abbot Weeks has summoned you back to the abbey."

Brother Benedict's face shifted through several different expressions in quick succession. Curiosity and excitement first, swiftly followed by sorrow. Lacey wondered if he was just as unhappy about the thought of leaving here as she was about him going.

She pushed those thoughts away as she took the wooden crate containing the scepter over to the table and opened up the box.

Crispin Noble approached and picked up the gold scepter gently.

"What are you checking for?" Lacey asked him.

"The inscription," he replied, peering intently at the scepter. "I think I found something in my research related to the Latin phrase. If I'm right, the treasure hunter may very well have been murdered because of it."

Lacey frowned, confused. There was already a suspect sitting in jail accused of Greg's murder. It would only be a matter of time before Superintendent Turner and DCI Lewis wore him down in the interrogation room and squeezed a confession of murder out of him. And it had absolutely nothing to do with the scepter. Marcus Moyles was a chancer, someone who'd inadvertently stumbled upon an opportunity. He wasn't a smart man or a scholar. Not only would he possess zero knowledge about the scepter's existence, he'd also have no interest in a Latin inscription, surely?

"You're going to have to explain," Lacey said. "Because as far as I understand, Greg's murder had nothing to do with the scepter."

Crispin turned to face her, looking bemused. For a moment, it looked as if he was going to argue his point, but he must've changed his mind. Instead, he said, "Oh? My mistake," and turned back to his work.

Lacey let the curious exchange hang in the air between them.

"It's a good thing your thief ran off before they could get the safe open," Crispin said as he worked. "None of my photos had a clear enough view of the inscription."

Suddenly, Lacey faltered. How did he know about the attempted break-in at her store? She hadn't told him. Presumably Gina hadn't either. So how did he know?

Suddenly, a new theory popped into Lacey's mind. Crispin Noble had been the one to break into her store. He wasn't even supposed to be in town anymore.

A chill went through Lacey. She looked over at Brother Benedict. The monk must have had the same thought as her, because he looked suddenly very wary of the man standing at the desk inspecting the scepter.

CHAPTER TWENTY THREE

"It was you," Lacey stammered, backing away from the professor.

"What was me?" Crispin Noble asked, in a voice that suggested innocence.

But Lacey knew better. There was no way for the professor to know about the break-in at her store, let alone the extra details about the safe. He was feigning his innocence because he was the culprit!

Growing increasingly nervous, Lacey took another step back from him, close enough to Brother Benedict to feel his calming aura. She drew strength from it.

"You were the one who broke into my store," she accused Crispin Noble.

The professor's face blanched. He did not need to say another word for Lacey to get her answer. His guilty expression said it all. Sitting in front of her was the masked intruder who'd tried to steal the scepter from the safe!

"Now listen," Crispin Noble said, raising both hands in a stop gesture. "It's not what you think."

"Did you do it?" Lacey demanded again.

In response to her demand, the professor was becoming increasingly flustered. He wrung his hands nervously in front of him, looking so far from the thief she'd envisioned she briefly thought she must have made a mistake. That was, until he spoke.

"I—I, yes," he stammered. "Yes, it was me."

Anger raced through Lacey's veins. She exchanged a glance with Brother Benedict. Even without words she could feel the fury in his eyes and the anger of his feelings. The scepter was the abbey's only chance at keeping its outreach program operational—the very same program that had saved Brother Benedict from a life of misery. For him, this was personal, and Lacey was quietly relieved he'd taken a vow of pacifism. Had it not been for that, she was quite certain he would've lamped Crispin Noble!

The tension in the room was so palpable, it even affected Chester. He went back on his haunches, adopting a defensive pose, and began to emit a low growl.

"Let me explain," Crispin said.

"You think I want to hear your explanation?" Lacey challenged. "As if there's any way to justify an attempted robbery?"

But before he answered, a horrible thought overcame Lacey. Was Crispin also the person who'd killed Greg Ford? Were the theft and the murder connected?

Her mind began to race. As much as her instinct was to lay into this awful man who'd admitted to trying to steal from her, if Crispin really was the killer, then he was dangerous and she needed the cops here right now. And that meant keeping him talking until they got there.

Swallowing her anger, Lacey slid her hand into her pocket for her cell phone. "Did Greg offer you a deal?" she said, forcing out a measured voice.

Crispin shook his head. "It wasn't like that."

His eyes kept darting from Lacey to the monk to Chester and the door, as if assessing his chances of escaping. They were slim, Lacey decided, but that didn't stop her from thumbing the speed dial to Wilfordshire station into her phone in her pocket. She prayed her phone speakers were quiet enough not to be heard.

"Are you sure about that?" she asked, speaking calmly now. "Because he offered me one. A good one, too. Take the scepter and split the profits."

From her peripheral vision, she saw Brother Benedict shoot her a pained expression. Lacey wished she could tell him that she hadn't entertained Greg's offer for even a second, but she needed Crispin to believe she had if he was going to confess. If that meant Brother Benedict temporarily believing it too then so be it.

Crispin puckered his lips in a way Lacey took to mean yes. So Greg had approached him with the same deal. Only where Lacey had said no, Crispin had caved. And then what? Had the deal turned somehow sour, perhaps in a way that caused Greg to become violent, and Crispin to retaliate?

As she turned the theory over in her mind, her cell phone suddenly connected, and the muffled yet audible voice rang out. "Wilfordshire police? How can I help you?"

Crispin's eyes widened. Then everything happened all at once.

Crispin bolted for the door. Brother Benedict stepped in front of it, using his large body as a blockage. Meanwhile, Chester sprang up from his haunches and stood behind Crispin, and began barking loudly, incessantly. There was nowhere for Crispin to go. He was trapped between a monk and an English shepherd.

"Let me go!" Crispin cried. Then his eyes darted to the cell phone Lacey had removed from her pocket, the screen clearly showing it was connected to Wilfordshire Police Station. "Help! Help!" he screeched, directing his voice at the phone. "I've been kidnapped!"

Lacey quickly put the phone to her ear. "I need to speak to Superintendent Turner," she said hurriedly.

"Do you, ma'am?" came the bored, lazy voice of the lady on the other end.

Lacey tensed. Of course it would be the same receptionist who had it out for her!

"This is preposterous!" Crispin was yelling. "You can't keep me in here!"

He tried to shove past Brother Benedict, but to Lacey's astonishment, the monk shoved him roughly into the office chair, making it spin beneath him. Crispin had nowhere to run. He blinked up at Lacey, looking stunned.

"Please," Lacey continued into her cell. "This is important. I know who killed Greg Ford. I have him right here."

From where he sat in the office chair, Crispin Noble shot Lacey a pained and panicked expression. "You think I *killed* him?" he cried.

Lacey ignored him, trying to keep her focus on the telephone call, and her lifeline to the police. But there was so much noise—from Crispin's protests and Chester's barks, and now Gina knocking panickily on the other side of the door—that Lacey could hardly hear a word she was saying. But she got the gist of it. The receptionist on the phone was explaining that the detectives were too busy to attend to her, and she was using the same irritated voice she always did when it was Lacey who called. This call was pointless. She wasn't getting anywhere.

She hung up and called Beth's personal phone instead, praying her friend would pick up while on duty, not something she always did.

As she listened to the dial tone, Crispin continued with his anguished explanations.

"Look, I admit I tried to steal the scepter and that I was in cahoots with Greg Ford. But I did not kill him!"

"Why would I believe you?" Lacey demanded.

"Because it's the truth!"

"You tried to steal from a charity!" she cried back. "You're clearly a cruel and heartless individual."

Crispin looked stung.

Suddenly, the door flew open and in tumbled Gina. But to Lacey's astonishment, she was not alone. Superintendent Turner and DCI Beth Lewis came tumbling in with her. The sound of a cell phone ringing came shrilly from the female detective's pocket.

Everyone froze.

Turner took one look at the scene—of the man in the office chair being towered over by Brother Benedict, of Chester, teeth bared and in his pouncing pose—before sucking his teeth and glowering at Lacey.

"Why did I just get a call about a possible hostage situation?" he said, running a nervous hand through his shock of white hair.

Lacey pressed the red button on her phone and Beth's cell stopped ringing. She looked down at Crispin expectantly. "Are you going to tell him, or am I?"

The professor paused momentarily. "I'm the one who broke into the store," he said eventually, hanging his head with shame.

Superintendent Turner's eyebrows went up.

"And…" Lacey prompted. "Please tell the detective who you were teamed up with."

"Greg Ford…" Crispin mumbled, so quiet he was barely audible.

"And…" Lacey prompted again.

"And nothing!" Crispin cried. "That's it! I tried to steal the scepter for him. I DIDN'T kill him!"

Superintendent Turner looked at Beth. "Take Professor Noble to the station. He has some serious explaining to do."

Beth nodded and approached the man. She hauled him to his feet and manhandled him out the door. Everyone else followed, leaving Lacey and the superintendent alone.

As soon as they were gone, Lacey frowned at him. "Why aren't you arresting him?"

"Because," Karl replied, tersely, "the last person I arrested in relation to this case is now free. I'd like to avoid making any silly slip-ups right before my retirement, or I'll be teased at my party."

Lacey blinked with surprise, not just because of Superintendent Turner's uncharacteristic concern over being teased at his retirement party, but because of his revelation that the last person arrested was now free.

"I'm sorry, what?" she asked. "Do you mean Marcus Moyles has been released?"

He nodded. "Released on bail."

"But he confessed to trying to steal Greg's gold!" she cried.

"He did," Karl replied. "And yet surveillance footage from the Lodge shows him fast asleep at his table for half the night until his wife arrives and drags him home."

"He lied?" Lacey questioned, struggling to comprehend it herself. "Why?"

"Probably an alcohol-induced fantasy," Karl Turner explained. "A drunk dream. Delusions of grandeur. Whatever his reason for saying he did it, we have irrefutable proof he didn't."

Lacey was dumbstruck. If Marcus was innocent on all counts, then that could only mean the likelihood of Professor Noble being the killer became even greater. She shuddered at the close proximity she'd spent with a man who was capable of murder.

"But wait," she said, remembering something. "You said there was evidence of a break-in. A damaged door. How does that get explained?"

"That was… historic damage," Superintendent Turner said, his demeanor becoming suddenly shifty. "Ours, in fact," he added. His cheeks were starting to turn pink. "The manager there kindly reminded us of the time our SWAT team swarmed the place…"

Lacey gasped, remembering the arrest of Eldritch Von Raven—a case of mistaken identity—and just how furious Suzy had been with her over the whole thing. "Oh. That."

"Exactly," Superintendent Turner replied, coughing awkwardly into his fist.

Lacey turned it all over in her mind. "So Marcus has nothing to do with anything?"

"Absolutely nothing."

"So that makes Crispin Noble the prime suspect?"

"It does."

She nodded slowly, digesting it all. She couldn't help but feel slightly stung that the man had duped her. She'd welcomed him into her store in good faith and he'd betrayed her.

"I guess having a suspect in custody isn't enough to give me my wedding back. You'll need a solid confession before you let me leave town, right?"

Karl peered down at her from his six-foot-high frame. "Lacey, you can have your ceremony," he said calmly.

"What?" Lacey gasped. Was this another one of his jokes? "Are you being serious?"

"Yes. The case is as good as solved."

Lacey was so thrilled, she threw her arms around Karl. He chuckled as she clung to him, and patted her back awkwardly.

"Thank you," Lacey cried.

Superintendent Turner harrumphed and removed her arms from around his neck.

Lacey wiped the tears of happiness from her eyes. "I don't know how to ever repay you." Then she paused. "Yes, actually, I do. You should come."

Karl's eyes widened. "Come to…"

"My wedding," she blurted. Maybe she was just delirious with joy, but she suddenly wanted the big polar bear of a man at her wedding. It felt like the perfect way to draw a line under the sand of their previously antagonistic relationship.

Karl's gray brows flew up to his hairline. "You're inviting me to your wedding?"

"Yes!" Lacey exclaimed. "We know each other pretty well these days, don't we, Karl? It's been a year since I first started making trouble for you. And since you're about to retire, I won't be that pesky, meddling woman getting in the way of your investigations anymore. I can just be a friend. Or an acquaintance if you prefer," she added hurriedly, in response to his near-panicked look at her mention of the "f" word. "One step at a time."

Karl was silent for a moment. Then he coughed, as if dislodging a lump of emotion from his throat.

"Sure, kid," he said, finally, his voice cracking. "I'll come to your wedding."

Lacey's heart soared. She was elated. Things were finally back on track! A suspect was in the jail. She'd been given the green light for the wedding to go ahead. And while she'd not been able to share her pregnancy fears with Tom, she *had* offloaded to Gina, and that had taken a significant amount of the burden from her shoulders. Everything was almost back to being okay.

All except one thing. She still had her mess of a family to deal with.

The dinner had been cancelled, and she'd successfully managed to use the murder and the scepter as excuses not to deal with them. But now the time had come to finally resolve that issue. It was finally time for the family reunion dinner.

CHAPTER TWENTY FOUR

Lacey's stomach was a knot of apprehension as she entered the restaurant. Not even the gentle piano music and soft lighting could calm her nerves. This was going to be one heck of an experience.

She approached the server's stand, knees trembling.

"I have a booking," she said to the woman waiting behind it.

Her eyes went past the server's shoulder apprehensively, scanning the dining area behind. The lighting was low, and among the dozen green-leather, curved booth–style seating areas, at least half of them were filled with guests. Lacey spotted her mom and Naomi at the far end, lit by a small candle on the table and a low-hanging, industrial-style light fixture hanging from the ceiling above. Frankie wasn't there. And, more importantly, neither was Frank.

"Oh. There they are," Lacey added, pointing them out.

"Right this way," the server replied, genially, collecting a menu for Lacey as she stepped away from the podium.

Lacey followed. She was relieved to have gotten there before her father, and was glad Naomi had made the wise decision to leave Frankie at Crag Cottage with Gina. It was time for the grown-ups to talk things through. Although, considering what had happened last time they'd all been together, Lacey suspected there'd be less talking and more yelling. She cringed in anticipation of an imagined future where all the diners she was currently weaving her way past were staring at her with astonishment.

"Here you go," the server said, gesturing to the spare seat next to Naomi.

Lacey slid into it. "Hi, guys," she said. "Thanks for coming."

Shirley didn't look best pleased. Naomi looked like she was already close to tears.

The server passed the menu to Lacey. "Are you ready to order?"

"Not yet," Lacey said. "We're still waiting for one."

Shirley scoffed. "And we might be waiting for thirty years if history's anything to go by."

The server frowned with confusion, and Lacey's cheeks grew warm. Shirley was already in a bad mood, and it was making her more tense.

"Perhaps you'd like to order some drinks?" the server asked.

"Yes," Naomi said rapidly. "Wine!"

"Of course," the polite server replied. "What type?"

"Just whatever you have that's strong," Naomi answered. "None of this eleven percent rosé stuff."

"She means what color," Lacey said under her breath. She was finding this all rather embarrassing.

"I don't care," Naomi replied. "Just as long as it has a high percentage. I need some Dutch courage."

Lacey looked up at the server and smiled sheepishly as she handed back the wine menu. "I guess we'll take a bottle of your finest, strongest wine in that case."

The server took the menu back off Lacey, trying her best to hide an amused smile at her unconventional guests. "Coming right up," she said, before hurrying away.

Lacey's toes curled at the thought of her returning to the kitchen and retelling the story to the cooks.

"So," Shirley began as soon as she was gone. "The forest ceremony is back on, is it?"

She sounded far from thrilled. Lacey frowned with confusion. "It is… I thought that was what you wanted."

"Yes, of course," Shirley replied bluntly. "I just would've preferred not to have spent all day trying to convince the harpist to bring her gold concert harp onto a sandy beach… She was quite rude about the change, by the way. Apparently the sand gets in the mechanism and the salty air can warp the soundboard or something like that. Not that it matters now. But I might leave off telling her we're back to the forest again for the time being. Let her stew for a while."

Lacey grimaced with guilt. "I'm really sorry, Mom. That can't have been very pleasant for you."

Shirley pouted. "I guess it doesn't matter now. All's well that ends well."

Lacey smiled with gratitude. "I am sorry though. I know it's all been a bit of a nightmare, and I appreciate everything you've done to try and pull this together."

"If the wedding's back on," Naomi asked, "does that mean the case has been solved?"

Lacey nodded. "All done. Well, pretty much. They have someone in custody, an archaeological scholar."

Naomi frowned. "A scholar? Not what you expect from a murderer."

"No," Lacey replied, conjuring an image of the professorial Crispin Noble in her mind's eyes—gray duffle coat, nerdy black and yellow striped scarf. "Or a Hufflepuff…"

For the first time since his arrest, something about Crispin being the murderer didn't quite sit right with Lacey. But she forced the thought away. It was over to the detectives now to get a confession out of him. She'd done her part.

Shirley opened her mouth—about to offer her two cents on the case, no doubt—but stopped as her eyes went over Lacey's shoulder. Lacey turned in her chair to see Frank at the podium talking to the server.

Lacey's heart skipped a beat.

"He's here," she said, turning back to her family.

Naomi immediately began to fidget in her seat. She drummed her fingers nervously on the table top, her gaze darting all around the restaurant. "Where's the wine?" she muttered.

Lacey could tell she was nervous about the meeting with her long-lost father, and she felt sympathy for her sister.

"Good evening," came Frank's voice from beside them.

Everyone turned to face him.

"Hi, Dad," Lacey said, jumping up. It was for the best if she was the leader here. She was the person on the most neutral ground, after all, the one who actually wanted them all to come together.

Frank kissed her cheek. "Hello, darling." He looked past her to Naomi and Shirley, neither of whom had moved a muscle. "Hi, ladies," he tried.

Shirley averted her eyes with a pout. Naomi's bottom lip quivered.

It was a cold welcome, and Frank's expression dropped, causing a knot of apprehension to tighten in Lacey's stomach. She offered him a smile of encouragement and lowered herself back down to sitting. Frank slid into the space beside her, and a tense silence fell over the table.

How many years had it been since all four of them had sat around a table like this? Lacey wondered. And then, with curiosity, she wondered whether everyone else was thinking the same thing?

Just then, the server returned to the table with the bottle of wine. "Oh look," she said, in a friendly manner as she gently put it on the table. "You're here. And it didn't take thirty years after all."

Lacey's stomach plummeted. Her father's face fell. Naomi gasped and put her hand up to her mouth. Shirley seemed so stunned she didn't even react.

The server didn't seem to notice that she'd completely put her foot in it. She laid out the wine glasses, one in front of each of them. When she got to Naomi she said, "This is the strongest wine I could find. I hope fourteen percent gets you through."

Lacey cringed, all the way from her toes to the tips of her hair. Naomi went immediately red and buried her head into her hands. Frank gazed at her with a hurt look on his face. He was no fool—it was obvious she'd asked for the strongest wine to get through the meal.

This time, Shirley did react. She snorted out a tense kind of laugh, and the server looked at her. Finally, the server took in all the tense, stunned expressions around the table.

"I'm sorry, did I say something wrong?" she asked, looking suddenly worried.

"No, it's fine," Lacey said, hurriedly.

Shirley let out another snort of laughter. "Nothing that hasn't already been said before."

"Mom, please," Lacey warned under her breath.

The server looked at them all, seemingly finally understanding that this was more than just your usual family meal out, that there was some unspoken tension going on. "I'm sorry," she said rapidly before scurrying away without taking their orders.

Lacey felt terrible for her. It wasn't her fault. She thought she'd been making friendly conversation, not dredging up old wounds.

"I owe you all an apology," Frank suddenly blurted.

Every pair of eyes turned to him with shock. No one had expected him to cut straight to the chase like that, and it took them all by surprise.

"And an explanation."

His expression was stolid, but Lacey could read the pain and regret in his eyes. Her heart skipped. Was this it? The moment she finally learned what had lured her father away from her all those years ago?

"Here?" she asked, looking all around her. "Now?"

Frank nodded. "It's time."

Shirley grabbed the wine bottle and poured herself a glass, before promptly downing it. "This will be good," she said.

But suddenly, Naomi leaned forward and laid her hand on top of her father's. "Can we just leave it at an apology?" she asked.

Frank looked stunned. He glanced down at her hand on his, then turned his so it was palm up and squeezed. "You...don't want to know why?"

She shook her head. "Not right now. Not right away. I'm just... I'm not ready yet. Mom might be. Lacey might. But I'm not. So can we just eat this meal and catch up, and then go to the wedding tomorrow and drink too much prosecco and dance to the macarena? And then, once I'm home and the dust has settled and everything is back to normal, then can we talk about it? One on one."

Lacey felt a surge of pride for her younger sister's courage. Accepting Frank even existed had been hard enough for her. And now standing her ground and expressing where she was at so eloquently was a moment to behold.

"But—" Frank began.

"I agree," Lacey blurted, throwing her own opinion into the fray.

Whatever it was that had lured her father away from her all those years ago—be it the love of another woman, the cliffs of Wilfordshire, or something darker and more sinister—knowing would hurt. And knowing it now, just before he was to walk her down the aisle, would bring nothing but pain.

"I don't know what to say," Frank said.

Lacey thought of the strong silent presence of Brother Benedict, who had put her at ease by removing all the social pressure of making conversation and keeping up appearances. She grabbed her father's other hand and squeezed.

"Say nothing," she said. "That's what we're asking. There's nothing you need to say. We just want you to be present. Just be here."

Frank looked astonished. His eyes darted from his elder daughter's hand to his younger daughter's and back again, as if he couldn't truly comprehend what he was seeing. He began to tear up.

He opened his mouth to speak, and then, as if taking heed of Lacey's words, he closed it again and let out a long exhalation. It sounded like he'd released a breath he'd been holding for a very, very long time. Perhaps for thirty years.

"I want to know," Shirley suddenly said from across the table. "But we can talk, just the two of us. After. Without the girls. And I promise not to tell them what you tell me. They deserve to hear it from you."

Everyone looked at her. For the first time, she seemed to understand that this was greater than her. That on this one occasion, she had to put others' needs before her own.

"Then that's what we'll do, Shirley," he said with a firm nod.

CHAPTER TWENTY FIVE

"How was he?" Naomi asked Gina as she and Lacey returned to Crag Cottage after the meal.

Gina gestured to the sleeping Frankie on the couch. "A delight. He helped me feed the sheep, prune the bushes, rake the soil. He's quite the gardener."

"That will be his next obsession," Naomi said with a loving smile. She went inside to rouse her son. "Come on, sleepyhead. Let's get you up to bed."

Frankie took her hand and they left the room together.

"I'm going to bed too," Shirley said from the doorway.

Lacey approached her. "Thank you, Mom," she said. "I know the last few days have been really tough on you. And I really appreciate you agreeing to leave all the heavy talk until after the wedding."

Shirley nodded. "I just want you to have the perfect wedding you always deserved. To the perfect man." She swept Lacey's dark curls behind her shoulder with a tender hand. "I'm proud of you, Lacey, for being brave enough to trust again. I never could."

She sounded wistful. Lacey felt for her. She'd never gotten over Frank's betrayal.

Shirley headed toward the living room.

"Mom?" Lacey said. "Aren't you going to bed?"

"Yes, in here," Shirley replied. "I don't think you should have to sleep over at Gina's on the night before your wedding. You take the guest room."

Lacey smiled. "Thanks. Good night, Mom. I'll see you in the morning."

Shirley went inside the living room and shut the door softly.

Lacey turned to Gina. "What a day," she said under her breath. "I have a LOT to tell you."

The two women headed into the kitchen.

"Want a drink?" Gina suggested as they entered.

"I'd better not," Lacey said, looking down at her stomach and thinking of the pregnancy scare. "You know. In case…"

Just then, Gina placed something on the counter in front of her. It was a pregnancy test.

Lacey gasped. “Gina!”

“I took the liberty to buy you one of these,” her friend replied with a grin. “I figured you’d be too busy today to find the time. I got the most accurate test, so it will definitely be right.”

“Gina!” Lacey exclaimed. She picked it up and hugged her. “Thank you!”

“Yes, well, the pharmacist gave me a right look, the cheeky cow!” Gina replied.

Lacey recalled the jokes the pharmacist had made to her about her having “baby brain.”

“She’s not the most professional woman I’ve ever met…” she commented. She looked at the test in her hand. “I’m going to do it.”

“Now?” Gina asked. “The night before your wedding?”

Lacey nodded. “Yes. There’s no time like the present.” She thought of the family reunion dinner that had gone so differently than she’d anticipated. “Sometimes you just have to be brave and take the plunge, because the outcome might surprise you.”

Gina headed for the door. “In that case, I’ll see you tomorrow.”

“Actually,” Lacey said, stopping her in her tracks. “Do you think you could stay for a little bit? Until it’s done? I could use the moral support.”

Gina gave her a supportive nod. “Of course, dear. I’ll stay as long as you want.”

Making sure she was as quiet as possible so as not to wake Naomi and Frankie sleeping in the master bedroom, Lacey tiptoed up the stairs—earning a curious look from Chester as she crossed the landing to the bathroom and closed the door silently behind her.

Her heart pounded as she took the test, her mind turning over and over again.

Pregnant, not pregnant, pregnant, not pregnant…

With all the symptoms she’d been experiencing—the nausea, the fatigue, the forgetfulness—along with the second gray line and pharmacist’s words, she couldn’t help but think that she probably was. Which would be an interesting start to married life to say the least. She’d heard of honeymoon babies before; this would be preemptive to say the least!

Securing the test in its container, Lacey paused at the bathroom mirror momentarily, picturing herself as someone’s mother. Could she rise to the challenge? Could Tom? And more importantly, would he want to?

Swallowing her emotion, Lacey crept back down to Gina in the kitchen. Her friend was sitting at the table. She'd brewed a teapot of chamomile tea, and the delicate fragrance permeated the air.

Lacey took a deep, steadying breath and set the test down on the table in front of them. She took her seat.

"Now we wait," she said.

The two women stared at the test in silence. It was very tense.

The first pink line appeared.

And then… nothing.

No second line. Not even a faint gray squiggle. It was irrefutable. The test was negative.

A rush of emotion went through Lacey—shock, relief, and then just the smallest hint of disappointment. It was the latter of those emotions that took her most by surprise.

Gina turned to face her. "It's negative, hon," she said, gently.

"I guess those symptoms were just stress after all," Lacey murmured in reply, her eyes fixed on the solid pink line.

"You okay?"

"Yes," Lacey said, as the reality started to sink in and her initial feelings began to subside, allowing her true thoughts to solidify. She looked at Gina. "I'm relieved. If Tom and I decide to have kids, I want it to be just that: a decision."

She thought of Tom. He'd be at home right now, keeping out of sight as was tradition.

"Is it strange that I wish I was with Tom right now?" Lacey asked Gina.

"Not at all," Gina told her. "But you do know it is very bad luck!"

They laughed.

Finally, Lacey could really put all that anxiety out of her mind and look forward to the big day tomorrow, the wedding of her dreams, the day she became Lacey Forrester.

CHAPTER TWENTY SIX

The next morning, Lacey woke feeling refreshed. Better rested than she had in years.

At the foot of the bed, Chester stirred at her movements, and Lacey suddenly realized how quiet the house was. Not quiet in the sense that everyone was sleeping, but completely silent, as if the whole world had been muted.

Lacey immediately knew what that absence of noise meant.

Her heart skipping, she jumped out of the guest bed and ran to the window, pulling open the curtains to discover the whole garden was blanketed in snow.

Her heart soared. It was truly happening! She was going to get the wedding of her dreams!

She grabbed her bathrobe and pulled it on as she ran out into the corridor.

"It's SNOWING!" she bellowed at the top of her lungs.

Chester followed after her and started to howl.

A flurry of activity came from behind the master bedroom door; someone was jumping out of bed, running to the window and drawing back the curtains, and then racing to the door.

The door flew open and out came Frankie, in his pajamas, his ginger curls all over the place.

"It's SNOWING!" he cried, racing over to Lacey.

He grabbed her hands and they jumped up and down on the spot, crying, "It's SNOWING! It's SNOWING!" over and over again. Chester began to howl.

Naomi appeared in the doorway, bleary-eyed, her dark hair a mess.

"Shhh!" she said.

Then from the bottom of the staircase, Shirley's voice sounded. "Will you please stop shouting!"

But Lacey didn't stop. She felt like a child all over again.

Just then, there came a pounding at the front door. Lacey stopped jumping, and she and Frankie peered over the banister as Shirley went to answer it. In hurried Gina, bringing a flurry of snowflakes and a snow-covered Boudica with her.

"It's SNOWING!" she cried up the staircase.

“Not you too,” Shirley muttered, retreating back into the living room.

Chester poked his nose through the banister and barked. Down below, Boudica shook herself, making snowflakes fly off her coat, and barked in reply.

Gina hurried up the staircase, two steps up at a time, joining Frankie and Lacey on the landing. They all grabbed hands and bounced around in a circle.

“It’s snowing, it’s snowing, it’s snowing!” they sang, while the dogs howled along.

“We should make a snowman,” Lacey said, breathless with excitement. “Or drive up to the hills and go sledding!”

Gina took her by the shoulders. “Lacey, darling. Have you forgotten? It’s your wedding day! There’s no time for snowmen or sledding!”

“What about snow angels?” Frankie asked.

Gina shook her head. “We can’t ruin Aunty Lacey’s hair!”

Lacey huffed. “Well, I suppose marrying the man of my dreams is the only legitimate reason not to play in the snow. But it better still be there when we’re done. Can you imagine how fun the reception will be at the Lodge if there’s snow?”

“Let’s think about that after, shall we?” Gina replied.

She ushered Lacey into the bedroom, where Naomi was lying flopped face down on the master bed. Frankie followed, the dogs coming in after him.

“Sorry, Chicken,” Gina said. “This is the dress-up room now.”

Naomi immediately pinged up to sitting and gasped. “Is it time to see the dress?” she squealed, suddenly wide-eyed and eager.

“Yes!” Lacey cried. “Well, almost. We need Emmanuel to pick up Frankie and take him to the boys’ house, first.”

She went over to the French doors and peered through the white curtains at the driveway below. Right on time, a car pulled up along the pathway and drew to a halt on the driveway. As Emmanuel hopped out from the driver’s seat, Lacey noticed Finnbar in the front passenger seat, and the figure of Brother Benedict in the back. She grinned to herself. She’d relayed the update over Crispin Noble to Abbot Weeks, and though he still wanted his monk to come back to the abbey, Brother Benedict had made it very clear he was determined to stay put in Wilfordshire with Lacey until the work was done. And that meant he was coming to her wedding too!

Emmanuel came striding to the door and knocked.

"Frankie!" Shirley called up the stairs. "Your chariot awaits!"

Frankie quickly gathered up his things, running like a hurricane around the room. Then he quickly kissed Naomi's cheek, then Lacey's cheek, then even Gina's cheek.

"See you there!" he cried, excitedly, before running out of the room.

The sound of his footsteps thundered down the staircase. Through the window, Lacey watched him streak across the driveway and leap into the waiting car.

Of course, she thought. He was excited about another car trip, and having another person to ask car-related questions to!

From behind, Naomi clapped her hands sharply. "Come on, Lacey. Dress time! I'm dying to see it!"

Lacey grinned and ran giddily over to her closet. She got out the dress and quickly stripped out of her night clothes. Gina helped her into her dress.

"Oh Lacey!" Naomi squeaked from the bed. "You look amazing."

Lacey looked at her reflection, smoothing her hands over the fabric. She was thrilled that everything had come together at the last moment. The murder was solved. Her big day was here. Her family was finally civil. The pregnancy question was put to rest. And the scepter was safe.

Just then, there was a rap at the door, and everyone looked over to see Shirley enter holding a tray with a French press and mugs on it.

"I thought we could do with some caffeine," she said.

Then she caught sight of Lacey and halted. Her eyes filled with tears. Gina rushed over and took the tray from her, since she appeared so stunned by the sight of her daughter in her wedding gown she seemed to have forgotten all about it.

"Lacey!" she gasped, literally not even noticing Gina take the heavy tray from her hands. "You look beautiful!"

Lacey smiled. It wasn't often Shirley showed such tender displays of affection. But over the last couple of days, her mom had really stepped up.

"How are you doing your hair?" Shirley asked, coming over and immediately sweeping Lacey's hair up off her neck and piling it on her head.

"I was going to wear it down," Lacey replied.

"Down?" Shirley cried. "Goodness! No. You can't wear it down. Here."

She reached into her pocket and brought out one of her hair clasps. Before Lacey could even protest, Shirley had twisted her hair in a complicated way and clasped it into place with the clip. The result was actually very pleasing.

Lacey watched her reflection as she inspected the up-do. “I like it,” she said, pleasantly surprised and impressed by her mom’s secret talent.

Gina slid the coffee tray onto the vanity table and came over. “That can be your borrowed item, Lacey.”

Lacey frowned. “My what?”

“Your borrowed item. You know: something old, something new, something borrowed, something blue?”

Of course her superstitious side would come out in force today of all days.

But when Lacey remained blank, Gina’s expression turned to a look of absolute horror. “Oh Lacey. You’re not doing it, are you?”

“I wasn’t planning on it,” Lacey confessed.

“Oh but you must!” Shirley said, joining Gina’s side.

“Yeah, come on, Lacey,” Naomi cajoled. “It’s tradition.”

Lacey bit her lip. “Well, the dress is old, because it’s vintage. And the hair clasp is borrowed.”

“These are new,” Gina said, grabbing a pack of bobby pins.

“Then it’s just something blue left to go,” Naomi said.

“I have an idea,” Lacey said, clicking her fingers. “I still have that necklace from Penrose Manor with a sapphire gem on it.”

“Yes!” Gina cried, clapping. “That’s perfect! And it will look beautiful with your dress.”

“Yes, but there’s one problem,” Lacey said. “It’s locked in the safe at the store. If I don’t have time to make snow angels, I hardly have time to drive to work.”

But all the women exchanged glances.

“It’s not *that* far,” Shirley said.

“And you don’t want to jinx your wedding,” Gina added.

“And it will make you look like a princess,” Naomi finished.

“Fine,” Lacey cried. “I’ll be right back. No one do anything crazy while I’m gone.”

She hitched up her wedding dress and motioned for the door.

“You’re not going out in your dress, are you!?” Gina exclaimed from behind.

“I’ll be ten minutes at most!” Lacey cried.

“You might break it,” Naomi protested.

"It's not made of glass," Lacey refuted. "And it'll be quicker than taking it off and putting it back on again."

She whirled out of the room before her mom got the chance to throw her own unwanted opinion into the fray.

Chester followed her down the stairs. She opened the front door and squeaked at just how cold it really was, before hurrying through the thin layer of snow to her car. She hopped inside and turned the heater on high.

"Just a quick impromptu detour to the store, boy," she told Chester as she turned the ignition.

The engine revved, and Lacey pulled out of her driveway.

As she drove down the hill, she wondered if this was a good idea after all. The roads had been gritted for the snow but the narrow winding paths were still difficult to navigate. She went as cautiously and slowly as she could. The last thing she needed was to get into a wreck on her wedding day.

When she arrived at the store, Lacey hurried into the back room where the safe was located. But she'd not taken even two paces inside when she immediately realized something was wrong. The padlock was gone—and the door was open.

Lacey gasped. Her first instinct was to swirl around to make sure there were no intruders present. Everything was silent and still.

She turned back to the safe and pulled the door open toward her. She looked inside and gasped.

The scepter was gone.

Lacey reeled back in shock.

"No!" she cried, staring at the blank space where the scepter was supposed to be. "How?!"

With Crispin Noble—the self-confessed attempted thief—currently locked up in jail, Lacey had assumed it would be okay to keep the scepter locked in the safe again. But evidently not. Somehow, someone had gotten inside. But who?

It wasn't Crispin—he'd spent the night in jail. He must've been working with someone. He'd admitted to being in cahoots with Greg Ford, so maybe teaming up with other crooks was part of his MO. And if his first partner in crime was dead, then it made sense he'd go out and find himself another one. The question was…who?

Lacey paced back and forth across the room in her wedding dress, her mind turning it over.

Just then, Chester stuck his nose in the safe and barked.

"Oh, right," she said, snapping back to the moment. "Good point. I almost forgot I was here to get the sapphire necklace."

She returned to the safe to retrieve the blue sapphire necklace of Iris Archer's. But as she pulled the beautiful diamond necklace out, her eyes fell to some of the other treasures glittering at the back of the safe. Among the various jewels and diamonds were pieces of gold.

"Wait..." Lacey said, as something started to come to her mind. "Greg had gold. He was a self-confessed treasure hunter. He wanted to get the scepter so he teamed up with Crispin to try to steal it... Perhaps he teamed up with someone else before when he tried to get a hold of the gold?"

Her mind turned as she found herself returning to her very first theory. That the murder had been over the gold after all.

"Jacobite gold," Lacey said aloud.

Then suddenly, she gasped. Because the final piece of the puzzle had fallen into place in Lacey's mind. There *was* a third person—the killer—but they hadn't been on Crispin Noble's team. They'd been on Greg's.

Greg Ford had a partner in crime. Or at least, an *ex*-partner in crime. Someone associated with the Jacobite gold.

And that's when it hit Lacey.

Cousin Harry.

The lake dredger from Lochaber, Scotland. The confident, rich man who drove a yellow sports car and bragged about his business accomplishments. Tom's so-called cousin who appeared out of nowhere. He was just like Greg Ford—arrogant, braggy, self-centered—and that was because... because they were partners!

Her mind raced as she turned it all over. She pictured the pair of them in Harry's yellow sports car, a partnership of thieves, crossing from Scotland to England, faking identities, stealing treasure, and evading detection.

So what happened to cleave them apart? To cause one to end up dead? Had Greg gotten too bolshy? Perhaps he'd stolen the Jacobite gold and left Harry out to dry? Whatever had transpired between the two former partners, only one of them was still alive, and Lacey was certain he'd been killed by the other's hand...

She leapt into action, racing out the back room and into the office to get the phone. She dialed Tom, her hands trembling with anxiety.

"Lacey?" he cried as he answered. "How's it all going your end? We're all tuxedoed up and raring to go!"

There was a lot of noise in the background. Lacey could hear Frank's jolly singing, Frankie's hyperactive giggling, and Emmanuel's polite but loud chatter. She strained to hear.

"Is Harry with you?" she shouted, launching immediately into the issue at hand without wasting time on pleasantries.

"Huh?" Tom shouted in reply.

"Harry!" Lacey cried. "Is he there?"

"No. He's not here yet. I've got Frank, Emmanuel, Finnbar, and Frankie. Oh, and Brother Benedict. I assume you invited him."

He was clearly in high spirits but Lacey didn't have time for chitchat. "Where is Harry?"

"At his B&B, I presume," Tom replied, before laughing heartily. "No! I'm not having shots before my wedding!"

Lacey grasped the phone desperately. "Tom!" she shouted. "What B&B?"

"Carol's," he shouted back, and this time he sounded confused. "Lacey, what's this all about? Why are you so concerned about Harry all of a sudden?"

"It's nothing," Lacey told him. "I'll see you later."

She ended the call, her ears ringing from how loud it had been on the other end.

Lacey wanted to confront Harry, but she was torn, because her wedding was so soon! But the thought of Harry getting away with it, and the abbey losing their precious scepter, was too much to bear. Lacey couldn't let that happen. Wedding or none, she couldn't let Harry get away with theft and murder.

With a surge of determination, Lacey knew exactly what her next steps should be. She was going to catch a killer.

CHAPTER TWENTY SEVEN

Lacey hitched her wedding dress up as she raced into Carol's bright pink B&B and up to the counter.

"Is Harry here?" she asked, panting.

Carol looked her up and down with a frown of distaste. She'd always disliked Lacey, for absolutely no real reason, and now that Lacey was talking to her in a less than personable manner she seemed to be seething.

"Are you getting married or something?" she added, sounding surprised.

"Yes," Lacey barked. "And I need to hurry. Harry. Dark hair. Tall. Well built. Drives a yellow sports car. Is he here?"

Carol frowned even harder at Lacey's demanding tone, and pressed her lips into a thin line. "I don't have any guests called Harry checked in here. There is a gentleman who drives a yellow sports car, but his name is Adam Cole."

"Adam Cole?" Lacey echoed. "Dark hair. Tall. Well built?"

"Yes," Carol replied, as if she was speaking to an idiot. "And he drives a yellow sports car."

Lacey grabbed her cell phone and went online, typing in the name Harry had given them for his loch dredging company he supposedly owned. There was a whole section on their website about the Jacobite gold that had been found, but she skipped past that to the employees page and thumbed through. There was no Harry there. It was all a lie.

"He's not Cousin Harry at all!" Lacey cried. "He was using a stolen identity!"

That was why Tom hadn't recognized him when he arrived—not because he'd grown out of his ginger hair and small stature, but because he was an entirely different person! She remembered Tom's "coincidental" revelation that he'd just put photos on Facebook of their summer camp holiday to Somerset together all those years earlier, and realized that must've been how Adam Cole got a hold of the fake persona in the first place. It was all there in the public realm, for anyone with the guts to utilize it, just as Greg had done when he'd pretended to be Professor Noble. And it only further solidified Lacey's theory in her mind, about the pair of them stealing identities and chasing treasure across the county. The Jacobite gold found by the dredging company had been published online, and so too had her message about the scepter, albeit accidentally.

There was no doubt in Lacey's mind now that she was right. Adam Cole was Greg Ford's killer.

"Is Adam Cole here now?" she asked Carol.

Carol shook her head. "He checked out a few minutes ago."

Lacey didn't waste a second. She hurried back out of Carol's B&B and flung herself into her car. Chester looked at her curiously as she gunned the car to life and accelerated away from the curb against which she'd previously abandoned the car in her haste.

There were only two ways to get out of Wilfordshire, and both roads could be seen from the top of the hills. If she was quick enough, she might be able to catch sight of the yellow sports car.

But her need for speed was quickly impeded when she joined the back of a barely moving row of cars. Thanks to the snow, everyone was being extra cautious and driving at a snail's pace.

"Oh, come on!" Lacey exclaimed, thumping her steering wheel with frustration. She wasn't usually one for road rage, but this was ridiculous!

It was only then that she realized the edge of her dress was trapped in the door and was trailing along the mucky, snowy asphalt.

"You've got to be kidding me!" she cried.

Making a snap decision, Lacey took a side street. That was the benefit of being local—she could zip around all the back streets and avoid the main congestion spots.

The cobblestones of the street made her bump and judder as she raced along far too quickly. Her teeth chattered as she raced to the end of the road and took a left onto the service street behind the restaurants, then turned onto the road that ran parallel with the high street—the less attractive one where all the buses were routed along. She raced along, taking another service street in order to bypass the promenade road, which was likely very busy. Then, finally, she reached the road leading into the hills.

And immediately braked.

The road was packed! Hood to trunk, with a row of cars, and every single one had a sled attached to the roof.

Lacey peered out through her windshield up at the snow covered hills. There were hundreds upon hundreds of sledders.

Her mouth dropped open. It looked like every resident of every town in a fifty-mile radius had decided to come to Wilfordshire to sled!

"Dammit!" Lacey cried. There was no way she'd catch Cousin Harry aka Adam Cole now.

Just then, Chester started barking from the passenger seat. Lacey glanced over at him to see what he'd spotted. She was just in time to see a yellow sports car go racing the other direction, against the flow of traffic. It was heading for the promenade road.

"Clever dog," Lacey said, pushing the stick into drive and hitting the accelerator.

The chase was on.

Lacey gripped the steering wheel tightly and clenched her jaw. A high speed chase along the snow-covered promenade street seemed very ill-advised—on her wedding day, no less—but she was determined not to let "Cousin Harry" slip through her fingers once again.

She revved, accelerating even more in her attempt to catch up to the yellow sports car. A car honked as she swerved around it. And rightly so. Her driving was dangerous to say the least.

The yellow car passed through a green light ahead, which turned amber as Lacey approached. She put the pedal to the metal, weaving past the other cars that were slowing to a halt.

The light turned red, but Lacey careened right on through. A second later, the sound of sirens began to wail from behind.

"Shoot!" she cried, glancing into her rearview mirror.

She couldn't see a cop car, though she could hear its sirens, and knew it was for her. Then she spotted a blacked-out Merc coming at her from behind. It was Superintendent Turner and DCI Lewis.

They started honking. They wanted her to pull over because she'd run a red light, but that just wasn't going to happen. Lacey pressed on.

She came up behind the yellow car. Now it was her turn to honk. She blasted the heel of her palm onto the horn and a loud, constant beep rang out.

From the driver's seat of the car ahead, Lacey saw the man she knew as Cousin Harry turn. Then he sped up, pulling away from Lacey.

"Oh no you don't!" Lacey cried.

She floored it. But it was useless. Her secondhand Volvo was no match for the yellow sports car. Maybe the Merc could catch it?

Quickly, Lacey wound down the window and gestured with her hand for the cops to pass her.

The cruiser drew up alongside her, the window rolling down to reveal the stern face of Superintendent Turner in the passenger seat. He was wearing a black suit, dressed up, it seemed, for the wedding he was probably en route to. The wedding *she* was supposed to be en route to.

"Pull over!" he cried.

"That's the killer!" Lacey shouted back over the roar of the wind. She pointed through the windshield at the yellow sports car up ahead, as it began to shrink from sight.

"Pull over!" Superintendent Turner cried again.

Lacey cried with exasperation. Why did no one ever listen to her?

Then suddenly, there came an almighty squealing noise. Lacey looked back out the front and saw, up ahead, the yellow sports car squiggling all over the place.

"ICE!" Lacey cried.

It was too late. She felt her tires lose traction beneath her.

The Merc suddenly disappeared from view. She was spinning.

"Oh crap!" she cried, trying her best to keep control.

She bumped and juddered along, slipping and sliding, turning a full circle before suddenly hearing a loud thunk.

Then everything stopped moving.

Slowly, Lacey opened her eyes and looked up, surprised to still be in one piece. The back of her car had collided with the front of the yellow sports car. The Merc had smashed into the back. And there was Cousin Harry, aka Adam Cole, stuck right in the middle of his pursuer and the cops.

Game over.

The wreck had caused quite a crowd to form, and when Lacey jumped out of the car in her wedding dress, it caused quite a stir. And it only got worse when Superintendent Turner also leapt out of the car in his dapper black suit, his white hair gelled back in the style of a 1950s businessman. To anyone watching, it must have looked like they were the bride and groom!

"That's Greg's killer!" Lacey cried, pointing behind her at Harry as she slipped and slid across the snowy tarmac toward Superintendent Turner. "He's a con man. His real name is Adam Cole."

But just as she reached him, she suddenly felt coldness on her wrist, accompanied by the click sound of a lock. She gasped and turned back to see a silver metal handcuff around her wrist.

"What are you doing?!" she cried, looking at Superintendent Turner incredulously.

"I'm arresting you for dangerous driving, you lunatic!" he cried. "What's gotten into you? It's your wedding day. Why aren't you at home doing your hair or whatever it is women do?"

"Because *that's* the killer!" Lacey cried.

Karl wasn't listening. He started dragging her toward the Merc. Thanks to the snow and her fancy wedding shoes, Lacey couldn't even get enough traction to stop him.

"I'm telling you!" she cried, trying her hardest to dig her heels in. "You need to arrest that man! Check his car! You'll find a wooden box with a gold scepter in it!"

Beth was halfway out of the Merc now, speaking in her walkie-talkie, requesting a paramedic and police backup. She'd overheard Lacey's exclamations, frowned with interest, and trotted up to the sports car where "Cousin Harry" was sitting stunned inside.

He looked at the approaching detective. "Did you see that crazy lady? She was following me! Ran me off the road!"

"Step out of the car please," Beth said, stoically.

Adam Cole did as he was commanded, professing his innocence the whole time while jabbing an angry pointer finger in Lacey's direction. "She's a lunatic! She needs locking up, she does! In a hospital, I mean, not a station. She crackers! A total fruit loop!"

Beth didn't rise to his shouting. Very calmly, she said, "Is there anything inside your vehicle?"

"Like what?" Adam Cole replied, looking angry and flustered.

"How about you let me take a look?" Beth asked.

"There's nothing to see," he replied.

Beth opened the back passenger seat door, ducked inside, and reemerged holding the wooden crate.

"That's just wine," Adam Cole attempted to say. "Vintage wine, is all. Nothing to see."

"Sarge!" the female detective cried across the asphalt, holding it aloft to Superintendent Turner.

The detective halted and looked back over his shoulder. His face registered surprise, then intrigue. He looked at Lacey. "Don't. Go. Anywhere," he warned. Then he hurried across the icy road to see what his partner had found.

Lacey felt a surge of triumph. The scepter would corroborate everything she'd told them. She took a couple of tentative steps closer so she could see and hear better. She watched, with bated breath, as

DCI Lewis prized open the lid of the box with her fingers, and let out a gasp.

"She's right," the detective said to her partner. "It's the scepter, all right."

Both detectives turned in synchronization to look at Lacey. Lacey puffed up her chest with pride and grinned. She was elated. She'd done it. She'd solved this case, this time for real.

Detective Lewis clicked the button on her walkie-talkie. "We're bringing in a suspect," she said, before taking her cuffs from her pocket and roughhousing Cousin Harry out of the driver's seat of the bright yellow car.

"Adam Cole, I'm arresting you on suspicion of the murder of Greg Ford," she said.

As she continued reading the conman his rights, Superintendent Turner returned to Lacey.

"Well, well, well," he said, drawing to a halt beside her. "Lacey Doyle proves me wrong once again."

Lacey couldn't help but grin at him. "I told you, you ought to listen to me more often!" she said. She turned to look at the mangled yellow sports car, squished between her Volvo and the black Merc. "Shame about the car," she added. "I bet it was expensive." She turned back to Karl Turner and raised her hands. "Can I get these things off now?" she asked, rattling the cuffs. "I don't think they go with the rest of my outfit."

Instead of chuckling at her joke, Superintendent Turner let out a heavy, weary exhalation. "No," he said, shaking his head. "You can't."

Lacey blinked, perplexed. "But I just caught the bad guy."

"I'm sorry, Lacey, but you've left me no choice. I'm going to have to arrest you."

Lacey's eyebrows flew all the way up. "For what?" she whispered, breathless with shock. "I—I don't know what to say." Then she paused. "Wait. Is this a joke?"

"I wish," Karl replied. "But unfortunately, no. You ran this guy off the road. Blew a red light. Caused a three-car accident. And endangered many citizens. With this many witnesses, my hands are tied. You left me no choice. I *really* didn't want it to be this way."

"But—my wedding!" Lacey stammered.

Karl shook his head. He was clearly taking no pleasure in this. With a morose tone, he said, "Sorry, Lacey. The wedding's off."

CHAPTER TWENTY EIGHT

In the gloomy holding cell of the Wilfordshire station, Lacey sat on a hard plastic bench, head in hands. Her once perfect, one-of-a-kind boutique wedding gown was now streaked with muck, its hem blackened with grime, the long lace train torn.

She let out a sad, wry laugh as she realized Beth's warning had come true. Her meddling had led her here. Instead of getting married, she was sitting in a cell.

Just then, she heard a rattling noise and spotted the warden through the small window in the steel door. There came a clank, and a moment later, the steel door swung inward with a loud creak.

"The detectives are ready to speak to you," the warden announced, beckoning her over.

Lacey leapt to her feet. Though there was no chance of saving her wedding anymore, she still wanted to get out of the station as quickly as possible and reunite with her family and friends. They must be worried about her.

Lacey followed the warden down the corridor to the interview room, the whole walk listening to the swish of her tattered wedding dress as it dragged along the carpet. Good thing there were no mirrors in the station; she must look a state.

They reached the interview room and the warden opened the door. Then he turned to Lacey. "In you go."

Lacey swallowed her nerves and stepped inside.

Both Karl and Beth were waiting for her, sitting stone-faced at the interview table. They were both still in their wedding guest attire, and it occurred to Lacey then that they'd both been off-duty at the time of the chase. In fact, they were both supposed to be standing on the bride's side of her forest wedding ceremony instead of here, working overtime.

Karl gestured to the spare seat opposite them. "Sit, please," he said.

His tone was as unreadable as his expression. Lacey felt her nerves spike as she sat on the uncomfortable plastic chair. If anyone was standing on the other side of the one-way mirror, this must look like the strangest wedding ever.

"Well, Lacey," Karl Turner said. "You deserve a pat on the back."

"I do?" Lacey asked, surprised. That was not what she'd been expecting to hear.

"Adam Cole gave us a full confession."

DCI Lewis grinned. "You cracked the case, Lacey."

Lacey was stunned. She may have missed her own wedding, but at least she'd saved the day.

"So he was Greg's partner in crime?" she asked.

Superintendent Turner nodded. "They were con men. They'd trawl newspapers and forums to find artifacts, then turn up pretending to have knowledge, only it was a ruse to scout out the location and steal the item for themselves."

"We've linked the pair back to several unsolved cases in continents all across the world," Lewis added. "All of which had one common denominator. A yellow sports car."

Lacey's mind raced as she tried to absorb everything she was being told. "And the murder?" she pressed. "Adam killed Greg? But why?"

"That was because of the gold," Superintendent Turner explained. "A lake dredging company found the gold at Loch Arkaig. The papers ran a whole story on it. So our two con men went there to steal it. Only Greg decided to double cross his partner. He stole the lot. Screwed Adam out of his half and disappeared into the ether. So when Adam saw your post about the scepter on the archaeological society's forum, he knew his backstabbing partner would be coming for it."

"He tracked him down," Beth said. "Initially hoping to get the gold."

"But ended up killing him…" Lacey murmured.

Beth nodded in affirmation. "Said his fury got the better of him."

"He hung around in town after waiting for a chance to steal the scepter and recoup the financial loss from the gold," Superintendent Turner finished. "Which he achieved this morning, when he jimmied his way into your store through a loose bathroom window. He'd gained enough intel from pretending to be Tom's cousin to know your store would be unmanned because everyone was getting ready for your wedding, and that the streets would be quiet for the same reason, since half the vendors are guests. No witnesses to see him squeeze through the window."

"And the padlock?"

"He's a skilled burglar," Superintendent Turner said. "He knows the combinations people use. Tom's birthday, right? He said he guessed it first time."

Lacey's cheeks burned. She'd thought once before about how much information was online, and how much trouble it could get one into, and here was the proof. Greg Ford and Adam Cole had made an entire living out of it.

"Why did he confess?" Lacey asked. "Adam, I mean. It can't have been guilt. He seemed pretty chipper when he was pretending to be Tom's cousin. At least he definitely wasn't acting like a guy who'd just killed someone."

Superintendent Turner shrugged. "Only time will tell. But I'm sure he has a game plan."

Lacey sat back in her seat, taking a moment to absorb it all. "And Crispin?"

"He's just a sucker who got dragged into it by Greg," Beth said. "Looks like Mr. Ford didn't like getting his hands dirty. Without Adam, he needed someone else to do his dirty work for him. So he recruited Crispin."

"And me?" Lacey asked. "What happens to me?"

Superintendent Turner reached for his notebook and ripped out the first page. He handed it to Lacey.

Frowning, she looked down. She was holding a traffic ticket.

"Wait," Lacey said, perplexed. "That's it? A ticket?" She knew full well she should get way more than a simple fine and points docked off her license.

"Any self-respecting cop would keep you in the cell until you got bail," Superintendent Turner said. "And charge you for all your misdemeanors. And if my boss heard about me letting you go with just a ticket, he'd probably fire me." He paused, then smiled. "It's just too bad that this is already my last day. Pay the fine. Go to the classes. As long as you do that, you're a free woman."

"I've never been so thrilled to get a fine in all my life!" Lacey said, jumping up.

She couldn't help herself. She hugged them both.

"I'm really sorry about your wedding," Beth said as they embraced.

"Thanks," Lacey said, sadly. It was a bittersweet moment to say the least. She'd helped catch a killer, but at a huge personal cost.

Superintendent Turner uncuffed her and escorted her out to the reception area.

She went to the counter to get her belongings returned to her.

"One mobile phone," the receptionist said, handing the clear bag across to her. "One hair clasp. And one diamond necklace with a sapphire gem…" She raised her eyebrows with surprise, then finally looked up at Lacey standing there in her wedding dress. "Oh!" she exclaimed.

Lacey took her belongings with a sheepish smile. "Thanks."

Lacey scurried for the exit, turning on her cell phone as she went. She desperately needed to call everyone and let Tom know she hadn't abandoned him at the altar. But as she fiddled with her phone, she heard the sound of someone else behind her collecting their own items from the desk.

"One Hufflepuff scarf…"

Lacey swirled on the spot. It was Professor Noble. He must have just been released on bail.

"Crispin!" she cried.

The professor flinched and turned to face her. His face immediately turned beet red.

"Lacey? What are you doing here?" His eyes roved up and down her wedding dress. "Are you getting married?" Then he shook his head, as if none of that mattered. "I need to apologize to you," he said. "For breaking into your store. I don't know what came over me. That con man was very persuasive and—"

Lacey held up a hand to silence him. Because the moment she'd come face to face with him, she had been reminded of the last time he'd been in her store, when he'd rushed in during her call with Abbot Weeks claiming he'd worked out who the scepter belonged to. Suddenly, resolving that mystery mattered more to her than anything else.

"The scepter," she said, closing the space between them. "What did you find out about it?"

Crispin looked surprised for a moment. "The scepter?"

"Yes. The inscription. You said you'd worked something out."

"Oh, yes. The scepter belonged to a canonized monk who started the monastery. He was the patron saint of marriage, believe it or not."

Lacey's eyebrows shot up. "You're kidding me!"

"No," Crispin replied. "Ironic, wouldn't you say?"

Just then, Lacey heard the sound of the automatic doors opening and a blast of cold air came in with the sound of hurried footsteps. She looked over to see Gina rushing in.

"Gina?" she exclaimed, surprised.

"Oh, Lacey! Thank goodness I found you!" Gina exclaimed. "The cops called to say you were here."

"I missed the wedding," Lacey said, the full force of it suddenly hitting her.

"Actually," Gina said, grabbing her hand. "You didn't."

"Huh?" Lacey said, as her friend began to drag her out of the station and into the snowy streets.

"The caterers have gone," Gina explained. "And half the guests. But if you're willing to go with Plan B, Tom is."

"Wait, what?" Lacey said, digging her heels in. "Where is Tom?"

"On the beach, darling!" Gina exclaimed. "Waiting to marry you."

Lacey gasped.

"So? What do you say?" Gina prompted.

"As long as the most important people in my life are still there, then yes, of course!" Then she looked down at her battered dress. "Although I don't know if I can get married in this…"

"Don't worry," Gina said with a devilish glint in her eye. "I have a plan."

CHAPTER TWENTY NINE

Wilfordshire beach looked nothing like Lacey had ever seen it. It was covered in a light dusting of snow, and thanks to the thick snow-cloud cover overhead, the water was a light, milky gray color. It was so still, it almost had the appearance of ice.

Lacey had never seen her beach look this way before, and she realized with a sudden surge of delight that she'd now seen it through all four seasons in Wilfordshire. Wilfordshire was her home. It was only fitting that her wedding was taking place in Wilfordshire, and she was suddenly very happy that she was getting married in her town. Now it was time to fully put down her roots.

She glanced across to see the vendors of Wilfordshire High Street standing in a cluster waiting for her. Jane from the toy shop, Jens and Freya from the Coffee Nook, Brenda the barmaid from the Coach House. There was Ivan Parry, her former landlord, and Stephan and Martha from whom she rented the store. Nigel the valet from Penrose Manor. Percy Johnson, her grandfatherly antiques mentor. It seemed like everyone had turned out for her wedding, and Lacey was touched. Even Brother Benedict was there!

But there was still Lacey's tattered dress to worry about.

Just then, she spotted Emmanuel emerge from a small marquee tent in his full tux. He turned back and called inside, "Tom, you can relax. She's here." So that was the men's dressing room. Then she spotted another marquee set up closer to where she stood and realized they were both dressing rooms—one for Tom, one for her.

"Come on," Gina said. "Let's get you dressed."

She ushered her into the marquee.

Inside, Lacey discovered Sakura from the sushi place laying out party platters of bite-sized sushi, and a harpist in a green silk dress tuning a wooden Celtic harp.

Shirley suddenly hurried in through the marquee behind her.

"This was the best we could do," she said hurriedly. "Sakura agreed to provide some refreshments, and the other harpist was very angry about all the toing and froing from the forest to the beach—apparently concert harps are very sensitive to environmental changes—and she cancelled. But luckily, someone on our shortlist stepped up!"

Lacey remembered the young woman from the shortlist very well. Her repertoire consisted of Disney songs and songs from musicals. But none of that mattered to Lacey anymore. How silly to even care! After all she'd been through, having a harpist here on the beach on a snowy day was beyond a dream.

"Oh, Mom," Lacey said, swirling to face Shirley. "Thank you so much. This is perfect!"

Shirley visibly relaxed. "Oh. Good. I thought you might be disappointed."

"Disappointed? I'm thrilled!" She faced the harpist and Sakura. "Thank you so much for stepping in. Both of you. I'm so grateful."

"No problem," Sakura said, grinning. "I just took yours and Tom's usual sushi order and multiplied it by forty!"

The young woman in the green silk dress lifted her small wooden harp up. "I'll go and get into position," she said, before heading out the marquee with it.

As she exited, Taryn came in. She took one look at Lacey in her dress and screamed.

"Your dress!" she cried.

Lacey looked at Gina. "This is your plan? Get Taryn to fix the dress?"

"She did it once before," Gina explained.

Lacey couldn't argue with that. Taryn had turned the monstrosity of a secondhand wedding dress into a beautiful boutique piece, so if anyone could salvage the mess now, it would be her.

"What do you think?" Lacey said, biting her lip. "Think you can do something with it?"

"Sure… if you don't mind getting married in a minidress," Taryn said.

"Why not?" Lacey said with a chuckle. "None of this is how I planned anyway."

Taryn started tugging at her dress, pulling off ripped shreds of tulle, tutting as she worked. "How did you even…" she murmured grumpily as she worked.

Suzy appeared in the marquee next. She had a grave expression on her face, like something terrible had just happened.

"Um, Lacey…" she began. "Bad news. The detectives are here."

Lacey felt a wave of relief wash over her. "That's okay, they're invited," she replied, grinning.

"You invited them?" Suzy repeated, sounding baffled.

"Yup," Lacey said. "When I make my vows and become Lacey Forrester, I don't want any enemies. Karl and I made our peace." She cast a wary look at Taryn. "And I think Taryn and I have too."

Taryn looked up, disconcertedly.

"You're staying for the ceremony, right?" Lacey asked. "And the reception?"

For the briefest second, Taryn looked touched. Then she quickly wiped the look from her face, shrugged a shoulder, and said, "Yeah, sure, whatever."

She was feigning nonchalance, and Lacey couldn't help but smile. After all the animosity between them, she was glad to know they could put it all behind them and start afresh.

"Right," Taryn said. "That's the best I can do. Take a look at that."

Lacey stepped over to the mirror. Her elegant boutique dress had been transformed into a cool, sixties-style minidress.

"Taryn, you're a genius!" she cried, twirling around to get a good look from all angles. "I love it!"

Taryn smiled.

Just then, Naomi poked her head in through the marquee flap. "Lacey? You ready?"

Butterflies took flight in Lacey's stomach. She nodded.

Naomi came inside and Gina handed her the bridesmaid's bouquet, picking up her own. Then she handed a gorgeous dried flower bouquet to Lacey. "This is yours."

"Oh Gina," Lacey said, choking up. "It's perfect!" Then she swallowed her nerves and nodded. "Let's do this."

Lacey stepped out of the tent and heard the sound of the harp begin. Not Handel's *The Arrival of the Queen of Sheba* the original golden concert harpist at her forest wedding was going to play, but Pachelbel's *Canon in D* played on a small wooden Celtic harp by a nervous young woman. But Lacey didn't mind, not in the slightest. Because all those small details were meaningless after all. Just like it didn't matter that she was on a beach instead of in a forest, or that she was wearing a minidress instead of a long gown. The important thing was she was getting married today, to the love of her life, in front of all the people who mattered.

The long harp notes floated delicately around Lacey as she scanned the beach ahead of her and took in the sight of the lectern and the officiator standing beneath the flower adorned arch. It was her first glimpse of her father's construction and Gina's dried flower decoration.

It was beautiful, far exceeding her wildest expectations. Far more beautiful than any of the ones in the magazines Gina had been showing her for weeks. And more special, because it had been made by two of her most favorite people in the world. The sight of it brought yet another tear to her eye, and Lacey wondered if she was going to make it through the ceremony without breaking down.

And it was with that thought that her eyes found Tom. He was waiting at the front for her, hands clasped behind his back in an uncharacteristically nervous posture. Her focus homed in on him, taking in every minute detail of his gorgeous physique in his black tux. He looked just as handsome as the first moment she laid eyes on him, and any anxiety or trepidation she'd felt about stepping out here in front of all these people disappeared in an instant. Saying "I do" to Tom would be the easiest thing in the world for her to say. Because Tom was the love of her life, and she just couldn't wait to get their life together started.

Frank walked up to her. "You look beautiful, darling," he said.

"Thank you, Dad," Lacey said, touched.

"And I hope this doesn't count as over-parenting of me to say, but you must be freezing. Can I give you my jacket?"

Lacey couldn't help but laugh. And then shiver. It was colder than she anticipated. "Actually, that would be good. As long as you're okay."

Frank immediately shook off his black jacket. "Of course," he said, sliding it around her shoulders. Then he offered her his arm. "Ready?"

"I've never been more ready for anything," Lacey said with an eager grin.

She looped her arm through her father's, clutching it tightly for support. He hadn't been there to walk her down the aisle the first time, and Lacey was so thrilled to have him here to do it this time, when it really mattered.

Slowly, they began to walk through the gap between the chairs. It was less of an aisle, and more of a simple pathway in the sand between the chairs. But for some reason that made it all the more special to Lacey. She had walked these beaches with Chester a hundred times before. Never once had she imagined she'd one day be walking them for this purpose, for her wedding!

As she walked slowly, Lacey smiled at all the happy faces of her friends and family in the audience. Frankie was looking adorable in his mini tux. Tom's mom, Heidi, was dressed in a beautiful light blue dress and matching hat. Suzy was in floaty pink chiffon, the height of fairyness. Standing beside her was Lucia, looking stunning in a blood red bodycon.

In the row ahead, Lacey spotted Finnbar. He was almost unrecognizable since he wasn't in a plaid shirt, and had his chestnut hair neatly brushed. He smiled at her, his hazel eyes lighting up affectionately. Beside Finnbar stood Taryn. She was smiling at first, until she saw Frank's jacket draped around Lacey's shoulders, obscuring her creation, and glowered. Then Lacey spotted Beth with her honey blond hair twirling loosely around her shoulders like Cinderella, and Karl with his white hair slicked back again, no longer mussed from the car chase. Lacey felt a surge of joy as she looked into the eyes of all her friends and family, all the people who cared enough about her to be here today, celebrating, in these unusual circumstances.

Then she turned and fixed her eyes on Tom. The whole world seemed to melt away the moment his green eyes found hers.

They reached the front, and Frank gave Lacey a hug, before stepping to the side.

Lacey turned to face Tom. She couldn't help but grin. He flashed her his megawatt smile in return.

"You look amazing," he whispered.

"So do you," she replied with a grin.

Then in a hushed tone, he added. "I haven't seen Harry anywhere. Do you think he knows about the venue change?"

"Erm, about Harry…" Lacey said. Then she stopped herself. Now really wasn't the time to explain the whole situation! "Actually, I'll tell you later."

Tom looked momentarily perplexed, but then let it go. "Oh, I just realized," he said, looking her up and down again and taking in the sight of her new minidress. "I've never seen that dress before! No bad omens."

Lacey couldn't help but giggle.

The harp music finished and silence fell. The officiator cleared his throat, and to the background sound of breaking waves, he began to speak.

"Dearly beloved. We are gathered here today to join this man and this woman in matrimony."

Lacey felt her throat go completely dry. It was really happening!

The officiator turned to Tom. "Do you, Thomas Forrester, take this woman to be your wife, to live together in matrimony, to love her, to honor her, to comfort her, and to keep her in sickness and in health, forsaking all others, for as long as you both shall live?"

The whole time he spoke, Tom looked at Lacey. She could see such adoration in his eyes it turned her heart to gold. His lashes became wet with tears.

"I do," he said, his voice hitching with emotion.

Lacey's heart skipped as if in reply.

The officiary turned to Lacey next. As he spoke, she kept her gaze fixed on Tom as well, silently conveying her love and devotion to him.

"Lacey Doyle, do you take this man to be your husband, to live together in matrimony, to love him, to honor him, to comfort him, and to keep him in sickness and in health, forsaking all others, for as long as you both shall live?"

Lacey squeezed Tom's hands. They were trembling as much as hers. "I do."

The officiator beckoned for the ring bearer. Along trotted Chester, looking as proud as proud could be, with a red silk cushion on his back and the rings displayed on it. Lacey couldn't help herself. She burst out laughing.

Everyone watching laughed too, as if she'd given them permission to.

"Who's idea was that?" Lacey giggled, wiping the tears from her eyes. She looked around the audience and found Gina, the obvious culprit. But Gina was pointing at Frankie—who was supposed to be the original ring bearer. Well, if it had been his idea, then Lacey loved it even more.

"Tom, if you could please place the ring on Lacey's finger," the officiator said.

Tom bent down and picked up Lacey's ring, giving Chester a pet on the head to say thank you.

Then he took her shaking hand and placed the ring at the tip of her finger. He cleared his throat. "I give you this ring as a token and pledge of our constant faith and abiding love," he said, as he slid it into place.

Lacey's heart thudded. Her breath caught.

The officiator turned to Lacey. "Lacey? If you could do the same."

Lacey bent down to Chester. He looked so proud of himself, and so adorable, she couldn't help but ruffle his fur, just the way he liked. "Oh, you're a good boy, aren't you? And so handsome!" she cooed. The audience laughed with delight.

Lacey straightened up and placed the ring at the tip of Tom's finger. "I give you this ring as a token and pledge of our constant faith and abiding love," she said, sliding it into place.

Then she looked deeply into Tom's green eyes, her heart swelling with love.

The officiator smiled and spoke to the audience. "By virtue of the authority vested in me under the laws of the United Kingdom, I now pronounce you husband and wife." He looked at Tom. "You may kiss the bride."

A cheer went up from the audience. Tom swept Lacey into his arms and bestowed upon her the most tender, loving kiss she'd ever received. And in that moment, Lacey felt for the first time in her life that everything was truly perfect.

EPILOGUE

Lacey sat at her office desk, her eyes on the beautiful wedding ring now adorning her finger. She was supposed to be working, but she kept getting distracted by it. She'd never felt so at peace in her life. Everything felt just right.

She turned her focus to the computer screen. On it was displayed the research Crispin Noble had conducted into the Latin inscription on the scepter. The inscription related to the canonized monk, confirming its connection. So it was worth a lot, but not the millions "Cousin Harry" had killed Greg Ford for.

Lacey glanced over to the corner of the room, half expecting to see Brother Benedict there meditating. But he was long gone, having returned to St. Cyril's with the scepter. Lacey was going to miss his calming presence, but she was glad to know that she would see him again soon—he'd promised to come to the charity auction. It was the next big thing on Lacey's calendar, and she was looking forward to it. Even more so because afterward, she and Tom would be jetting away for their honeymoon in Paris. Three full weeks. She couldn't wait.

Just then, there came a knock at the door. Lacey turned in her chair as it opened, and in came Shirley, Naomi, and Frankie.

Lacey jumped up. They were here to say goodbye, and suddenly her heart ached for them. It had been a tumultuous trip to say the least, and Lacey had felt something shift between them all during it, almost as if they'd stepped over an invisible line. In a good way. She felt closer to them all now than she ever had her whole life.

"You're leaving," she said, going to them with her arms wide for an embrace.

All three folded into her arms.

"When am I going to see you again, Aunty Lacey?" Frankie asked.

She bent at the knees so they were eye level and took his hands. "How about the summer?" she said. "You could come and stay with me. Would you like that? Teach Chester some more tricks. Help out with the sheep. If you're lucky, there'll be lambs."

His eyes widened with excitement. "Yes!" He looked over to Naomi. "Can I, Mom? Can I stay with Aunty Lacey in the summer?"

"I mean, sure… if she'll have you," Naomi replied, gazing up at Lacey with querying eyes.

Lacey smiled. She may have had a close call with the pregnancy scare, but it had made her realize that raising a child would not be the disaster she always thought it would be. Especially if that kid was anything like her gingernut, car-obsessed nephew.

"I would love it," she said, ruffling his head.

Frankie punched the air, looking thrilled. "I'm going to go and say goodbye to Boudica," he said, darting out of the office.

The others went slowly out after him, taking their time to walk the corridors of the store into the main shop floor. No one seemed to be in a rush to say goodbye.

Lacey reached for Naomi's hand as they went.

"How are you?" she asked, softly. Of everything that had happened in their lives and over the course of the last few days, it was Naomi's well-being she worried about the most.

"You know what," Naomi said. "I'm actually okay." She smiled. "I kinda feel like a weight's been lifted, you know? I always thought I didn't want to know what happened with Dad. I expected the worst and just didn't want to know. But now I've met him, I think I can handle it. Because at least now that I know he's not some awful person, I can kind of accept that whatever he did back then was a mistake, or a bad decision, and not something deliberately cruel." She shrugged. "Does that make sense?"

Lacey squeezed her hand. "It makes perfect sense. And I'm really glad to hear that, Naomi. I'm looking forward to the future and us all moving on from this. I really think it's possible now."

"Me too," she said, smiling.

They made it out onto the main shop floor, where all the cases were stacked up by the door ready to go. Lacey saw Shirley's floral carry-on and felt a sudden, painful ache in her chest. It felt like she and her mom had made more progress during this trip than ever before. Lacey could sympathize with her more now, with the struggles she'd been through with her marriage and raising her children alone. She suddenly realized just how much she loved her, and how much she would miss her once she returned home to New York City.

She reached her mom and pulled her into a hug, feeling tears in her eyes.

"What's this for?" came Shirley's voice in her ear.

"I love you, Mom," Lacey whispered softly.

Shirley faltered. "I love you too, darling."

Just then, there came a honk from the streets.

"Our ride is here," Shirley said.

Lacey looked out the window. But instead of seeing a taxi as she expected, she was surprised to see her father's rusty, muddy, stinky cattle van idling in the middle of the street, belching smoke from its exhaust pipe.

"Wait…" Lacey stammered. "*Dad's* taking you to the airport?"

Naomi pointed to Frankie, who was playing with the dogs. "Blame that one," she said with wry affection. "Once he saw the damn thing there was no way he was going to let us leave without taking a trip in it. And Dad seemed happy to oblige. I think he might change his mind half an hour into the journey when Frankie's already asked him every possible question about cattle vans there is to ask three times over!"

Lacey grinned. She had a suspicion Naomi was wrong about that. Frank would delight in telling the grandson he'd only just met about the cattle van, grateful for the safe, common ground they could bond over—not to mention having a legitimate distraction from Shirley!

They headed out of the store to the street, joining Frank.

"I guess it's goodbye then," Lacey said to her father.

Her heart hitched as he reached for her and pulled her into a warm, safe embrace. Then Lacey felt more arms join in, and realized it was Naomi, and Frankie, and then, finally, Shirley.

She took a long, deep breath, savoring this moment of togetherness. Her family wasn't fixed, not by any means. There was plenty of hard work in the future, of painful conversations and difficult revelations, but Lacey felt for the first time in years that they were going to be all right.

*

That night, at the cottage, Tom and Lacey sat together on the white couch in the living room, with Chester asleep on the rug before them. Tom, it turned out, was a dab hand at lighting fires, and for the first time since Lacey had moved into Crag Cottage, a roaring fire burned in the fireplace. It lit the room with a cozy orange glow. With the snow blanketing the lawn and the stars twinkling in the black sky, framed by frost on the window, Lacey couldn't imagine a more perfect moment.

Tom topped her wine glass with some more red. "To us," he said, clinking his glass against hers.

"To us," she replied. "To being married, and to finally living together!"

Tom chuckled. It had taken a little while for him to agree to move to Crag Cottage. He was very fond of his apartment in the middle of town. But when Lacey had suggested he rent it to Finnbar rather than sell it, it was as if a switch flipped in him, and he couldn't wait to leave and move into the cozy cottage on the cliffs with her.

"Shall we get another dog?" Tom said, snuggling in next to her. He sipped his wine. "Or a cat? Or we could be totally crazy and get a goat or something. We'd never have to mow the lawn again."

Lacey held onto him tightly, feeling so full of love she could almost burst. Then, "I had a pregnancy scare," she blurted.

Tom sat up. He peered at her, blinking. "What? When?"

"Just before the wedding," Lacey admitted. "It was negative. I'm not pregnant. But it gave me a false positive so for a day I really thought I might be."

Tom paused, letting it all sink in. "And how did that make you feel?"

"Honestly?" Lacey said. "Terrified. But… not in the way I expected. Because I realized it's not so much that I don't want kids, just that I'm scared of being a mother. Or specifically of being a bad one, and making the same mistakes my parents made. But when I did the second one and it was negative, I actually felt a little bit disappointed."

A small smile appeared at the corner of Tom's lips. "Oh really?"

She nodded.

"Well," he said, snuggling back in beside her. "I personally don't think it would be all that bad if it happened. We're pretty cool people, you and me. I think we'd make pretty good humans. And anyway, we've proved now that we can handle anything together."

Lacey snuggled in to her husband. "You're right," she said, with a contented sigh. "Whatever the future holds, we'll face it together."

NOW AVAILABLE!

AGED FOR MURDER
(A Tuscan Vineyard Cozy Mystery—Book 1)

"Very entertaining. I highly recommend this book to the permanent library of any reader that appreciates a very well written mystery, with some twists and an intelligent plot. You will not be disappointed. Excellent way to spend a cold weekend!" --Books and Movie Reviews, Roberto Mattos (regarding *Murder in the Manor*)

AGED FOR MURDER (A TUSCAN VINEYARD COZY MYSTERY) is the debut novel in a charming new cozy mystery series by #1 bestselling author Fiona Grace, author of Murder in the Manor (Book #1), a #1 Bestseller with over 100 five-star reviews—and a free download!

When Olivia Glass, 34, concocts an ad for a cheap wine that propels her advertising company to the top, she is ashamed by her own work—yet offered the promotion she's dreamed of. Olivia, at a crossroads, realizes this is not the life she signed up for. Worse, when Olivia discovers her long-time boyfriend, about to propose, has been cheating on her, she realizes it's time for a major life change.

Olivia has always dreamed of moving to Tuscany, living a simple life, and starting her own vineyard.

When her long-time friend messages her about a Tuscan cottage available, Olivia can't help wonder: is it fate?

Hilarious, packed with travel, food, wine, twists and turns, romance and her newfound animal friend—and centering around a baffling small-town murder that Olivia must solve—AGED FOR DEATH is an un-putdownable cozy that will keep you laughing late into the night.

Books #2 (AGED FOR DEAD), #3 (AGED FOR MAYHEM), #4 (AGED FOR SEDUCTION), #5 (AGED FOR VENGEANCE), and #6 (AGED FOR ACRIMONY) are also available!

Fiona Grace

Fiona Grace is author of the LACEY DOYLE COZY MYSTERY series, comprising nine books; of the TUSCAN VINEYARD COZY MYSTERY series, comprising six books; of the DUBIOUS WITCH COZY MYSTERY series, comprising three books; of the BEACHFRONT BAKERY COZY MYSTERY series, comprising six books; and of the CATS AND DOGS COZY MYSTERY series, comprising six books.

Fiona would love to hear from you, so please visit www.fionagraceauthor.com to receive free ebooks, hear the latest news, and stay in touch.

BOOKS BY FIONA GRACE

LACEY DOYLE COZY MYSTERY
MURDER IN THE MANOR (Book#1)
DEATH AND A DOG (Book #2)
CRIME IN THE CAFE (Book #3)
VEXED ON A VISIT (Book #4)
KILLED WITH A KISS (Book #5)
PERISHED BY A PAINTING (Book #6)
SILENCED BY A SPELL (Book #7)
FRAMED BY A FORGERY (Book #8)
CATASTROPHE IN A CLOISTER (Book #9)

TUSCAN VINEYARD COZY MYSTERY
AGED FOR MURDER (Book #1)
AGED FOR DEATH (Book #2)
AGED FOR MAYHEM (Book #3)
AGED FOR SEDUCTION (Book #4)
AGED FOR VENGEANCE (Book #5)
AGED FOR ACRIMONY (Book #6)

DUBIOUS WITCH COZY MYSTERY
SKEPTIC IN SALEM: AN EPISODE OF MURDER (Book #1)
SKEPTIC IN SALEM: AN EPISODE OF CRIME (Book #2)
SKEPTIC IN SALEM: AN EPISODE OF DEATH (Book #3)

BEACHFRONT BAKERY COZY MYSTERY
BEACHFRONT BAKERY: A KILLER CUPCAKE (Book #1)
BEACHFRONT BAKERY: A MURDEROUS MACARON (Book #2)
BEACHFRONT BAKERY: A PERILOUS CAKE POP (Book #3)
BEACHFRONT BAKERY: A DEADLY DANISH (Book #4)
BEACHFRONT BAKERY: A TREACHEROUS TART (Book #5)
BEACHFRONT BAKERY: A CALAMITOUS COOKIE (Book #6)

CATS AND DOGS COZY MYSTERY
A VILLA IN SICILY: OLIVE OIL AND MURDER (Book #1)
A VILLA IN SICILY: FIGS AND A CADAVER (Book #2)
A VILLA IN SICILY: VINO AND DEATH (Book #3)

A VILLA IN SICILY: CAPERS AND CALAMITY (Book #4)
A VILLA IN SICILY: ORANGE GROVES AND VENGEANCE (Book #5)
A VILLA IN SICILY: CANNOLI AND A CASUALTY (Book #6)

Made in the USA
Las Vegas, NV
19 March 2024

87457483R00111